Elsie's Young Folks

Elsie's Young Folks

Book Twenty-Five of
The Original Elsie Classics

Martha Finley

CUMBERLAND HOUSE
NASHVILLE, TENNESSEE

Elsie's Young Folks
by Martha Finley

Any unique characteristics of this edition:
Copyright © 2001 by Cumberland House Publishing, Inc.

Published by Cumberland House Publishing, Inc.,
431 Harding Industrial Drive, Nashville, Tennessee 37211.

Cover design by Bruce Gore, Gore Studios, Inc.
Photography by Dean Dixon Photography
Hair and Makeup by Calene Rader
Text design by Heather Armstrong

Printed in the United States of America
1 2 3 4 5 6 7 8 — 05 04 03 02 01

CHAPTER FIRST

IT WAS A LOVELY summer day, bright and clear, but the heat was so tempered — there on the coast of Maine — by the delicious sea breeze that it was delightful and exhilarating. The owner and passengers of the *Dolphin* had forsaken her more than a fortnight ago and since spent their days and nights at a lovely villa on shore there in Bar Harbor. Now no longer able to resist the attractions of the beautiful sea, most of them had come aboard and were sitting, standing, or roaming about the deck. "Oh, I'm glad to be in our dear sea home again!" cried Elsie Raymond. "Aren't you, Ned?"

"Yes, though we have been having a splendid time on shore in Bar Harbor."

"Yes, so we have. But as we expect to be back again in a few days, we needn't fret at all about leaving it."

"No, and we needn't even if we were going back to Woodburn, our own beautiful home. That is certainly a better place than this in the winter months, anyhow."

"But I'm very glad indeed to have a sail again," said Elsie.

"Brother Max says we'll soon see some places where they had sea fights in our two wars with England," remarked Ned with satisfaction.

"Oh, does he? I mean to ask papa or grandma to tell us about them!" exclaimed Elsie.

"Oh, yes, let's!" cried Ned. "But the men are now taking up the anchor," he added hastily, "and I must see that first. Come," catching his sister's hand and hurrying her along to a good position from which to view the operation.

That duly attended to, they sought out their grandma, who happened to be at the moment sitting a little apart from the others, and made their request. She smilingly consented to tell them all she could recall on the subject that would be interesting to them, and bidding them seat themselves close beside her, she began.

"Your father has told me that we are now going out to the extreme eastern point of Maine and of our country, for that matter. West Quoddy Head is its name now, but in very early times it was called Nurumbega. In 1580, John Walken, in the service of Sir Humphrey Gilbert, concluded an expedition to its shores and reached Penobscot River. In 1603, two vessels, the *Speedwell* and the *Discoverer*, entered the Penobscot Bay and the mouth of a river — probably Saco. About three years after that, two French Jesuits with several families settled on Mount Desert and founded a settlement called St. Saviour. But not long afterward, they were driven away by some English under command of Captain Argal, who considered them trespassers upon English soil. That, I think, is enough of the very early history of Maine for today, at least."

"Yes, grandma! But won't you please tell about the Revolution and the War of 1812?" pleaded Elsie. "Maine was one of the thirteen colonies. Wasn't she?"

"No, dear. She was considered a part of Massachusetts at that time and did not become a separate state until 1820."

"Oh, didn't people there care about the Revolution and help in it?" asked Elsie in a tone of grave disappointment.

"Yes, dear, they did. In a county convention in 1774, Sheriff William Tyng declared his intention to obey provincial law and not that of parliament. He advised a firm and persevering opposition to every design, whether dark or open, framed to abridge our English liberties."

"English!" exclaimed Ned in a half-scornful tone, at which his grandma smiled. Stroking his curls caressingly, she said, "Yes, Neddie, at that time—before the Revolutionary War—our people liked to call themselves English."

"But we don't call ourselves English now, grandma. We're Americans."

"Yes, that is the name we have given ourselves in these days, but we still consider the English our relations—a sort of cousins."

"Well, then, I hope we and they will never fight any more," said Elsie. "But, please, grandma, tell us something more of the things that have happened along this coast."

"In 1775," continued her grandma, "the British kept the coast of New England from Falmouth—now called Portland—to New London in continual alarm. They were out in every direction plundering the people to supply their camp with provisions."

"Here in Maine, grandma?" asked Ned.

"Yes, and in Connecticut and Massachusetts. They bombarded Stonington in Connecticut, shattering houses and killing two men. That was in August or September. In October, Mowatt was sent to Falmouth in Maine to get a supply of provisions from the people there and to demand a surrender of their arms. They refused and defied him. Then, after giving time for the women and children to leave the town, he bombarded it and set it on fire. More than four hundred houses were destroyed—nearly all the town, which then contained about five hundred buildings."

"What a cruel thing!" exclaimed Elsie. "I suppose they had to give up then?"

"No," said Mrs. Travilla. "So very brave and determined were they, that they repulsed the marauders and would not let them land."

"Grandma," asked Elsie, "didn't Arnold go through Maine with an army to attack Canada about that time?"

"Yes, about the middle of August, a committee of Congress visited Washington in his camp, and together they formed a plan to send a force into Canada by way of the Kennebec River to cooperate with General Schuyler, who was preparing to invade that province by way of the northern lakes. Arnold was well known to be brave. He had long been complaining of being ill-used upon Lake Champlain. Washington decided to silence his complaints, and knowing that this expedition was well suited to his talents, he appointed him to command and gave him the commission of colonel in the Continental army.

"The force under his command consisted of eleven hundred hardy men—ten companies of musketeers from New England as well as three companies of riflemen from Virginia and Pennsylvania. Those riflemen were command by Captain Daniel Morgan, who afterward did such good work for our country in her hard struggle for liberty. Arnold and his troops marched from Cambridge to Newburyport, where they embarked on transports that carried them to the mouth of the Kennebec. They went up that river in bateaux and rendezvoused at Fort Western, opposite the present town of Augusta. Now they had come to the edge of a vast and almost uninhabited wilderness."

"And they had to go through it, grandma?" asked Ned incredulously.

"Yes. They were very brave men, ready to encounter difficulties and dangers for the sake of securing their country's freedom. Two small parties were sent on in advance to reconnoiter, and the rest moved forward in four divisions— Morgan with his riflemen in the van. Arnold, who was last, passed up the river in a canoe."

"Didn't they have a very hard time going through that wilderness, grandma?" asked Elsie.

"Yes, very hard indeed—over craggy knolls, deep ravines, through creeks and ponds and deep morasses, sometimes paddling along a stream in their canoes, sometimes carrying them around a fall on their shoulders. Suddenly, at length, they came to a mountain covered with snow. At its foot, they encamped for three days. Then they went on again, but a heavy rain set in, sending down such torrents from the hills that the river rose eight feet in one night. The water came roaring down the valley where our soldiers were so unexpectedly and powerfully that they had scarcely time to retreat and get into their bateaux before the whole plain was flooded with water. Seven bats were overturned, and the provisions in them lost. Many of them became ill, too, by the storm and exposure, and so they grew sad and discouraged. Some gave up and went back to their homes, while Arnold went on with the rest. The rain changed to snow, and there was ice in the water in which the poor fellows had to wade to push their bateaux along through ponds and marshes near the source of the Dead River.

"At last they reached Lake Megantic. They encamped on its eastern shore, and the next morning Arnold, along with a party of fifty-five men on shore with Captain Nanchet and thirteen with himself in five bateaux and a birch canoe, pushed on down the river to a French settlement to get provisions to send back to his almost starving men. They passed seventeen falls, marching through snow two inches deep, and then they reached the Highlands that separate the waters of New England from Canada. But as it is of the history of Maine I am telling you, and Arnold and his band have now passed out of it, we will leave the rest of his story for another time."

"He did a good deal more for his country before he turned traitor. Didn't he, grandma?" asked Elsie.

"Yes, he fought bravely again and again. The great victory at Saratoga was largely due to him and in a less degree to Morgan."

"Daniel Morgan who commanded at the Battle of the Cowpens?" asked Elsie.

"The very same," replied Mrs. Travilla.

"Didn't some other things happen along this coast, grandma?" asked Ned.

"Yes, indeed, several things. In the war of 1812–14, there occurred a naval battle near Portland between the American ship *Enterprise* and the English brig *Boxer*. On the morning of the first of September in 1813, the *Enterprise* sailed for Portsmouth, New Hampshire, and on the morning of the third, she chased a schooner suspected of being a British privateer into Portland Harbor. The next day, she left that harbor and steered eastward looking for British cruisers. On the fifth, they discovered in a bay what Captain Burrows supposed to be a vessel of war getting under way. She was a British brig, and on sighting the *Enterprise,* she displayed four British ensigns, fired several guns as signals to boats that had been sent ashore to return, and, crowding canvas, bore down gallantly for the *Enterprise.*

"Seeing that, Burroughs cleared his ship for action, sailed out a proper distance from land to have plenty of sea room for the fight, then shortened sail and edged toward the *Boxer.* That was at three o'clock in the afternoon. Twenty minutes later, the two brigs closed within half a pistol shot, and both opened fire at the same time. The sea was almost quiet, there was but little wind, and that condition of things made the cannonading very destructive. Ten minutes after the firing began, the *Enterprise* ranged ahead of the *Boxer,* steered across her bow, and delivered her fire with such precision and destructive energy that at four o'clock the British officer in command showed through his trumpet that he had surrendered. His flag, being nailed to the mast, could not be lowered until the *Enterprise* should cease firing."

"And did she, grandma?" asked Ned.

"Yes. I do not think our men ever fired on a foe whom they believed to be ready to surrender. Captain Blyth of the *Boxer* was already dead, having been nearly cut in two by an eighteen-pound ball, and Captain Burrows of the *Enterprise* was mortally wounded. He had been helping the men to run out a cannonade, and while doing so a shot, supposed to be a canister ball, struck his thigh, causing a fatal wound. He lived eight hours and suffered terrible agony. He refused to be carried below until the sword of the commander of the *Boxer* should be brought to him. He took it eagerly when brought, saying, 'Now I am satisfied. I die contented.'"

"What did they do for a commander after their captain was so dreadfully injured?" asked Elsie.

"Lieutenant Edward R. M'Call took command of the *Enterprise* and showed great skill and courage," replied Grandma Elsie. "On the morning of the seventh, he took both vessels into Portland Harbor. The next day, the bodies of the two commanders were buried side by side in the same cemetery and with all the honors to which their rank and powers entitled them."

"Were both of the ships spoiled, grandma?" asked Ned.

"The *Enterprise* was not, but the *Boxer* was cut up in both hull and rigging," she replied. "The battle showed that the Americans exceeded the British in both nautical skill and marksmanship. Lossing tells us that a London paper, speaking of the battle, said, 'The fact seems to be but too clearly established that the Americans have some superior mode of firing, and we cannot be too anxiously employed in discovering to what circumstances that superiority is owing.'"

"I think the man who wrote that was feeling mortified that one of their vessels had been whipped by one of ours," remarked Ned sagely.

"Yes," said Grandma Elsie. "I think the nailing of their flag to the mast showed that they felt confident of victory. Cooper tells in his history that when the *Enterprise* hailed to know if the *Boxer* had struck, as she kept her flag flying, one of the officers of the British vessel leaped upon a gun, shook both fists at the Americans, and shouted 'No, no, no!' adding some opprobrious epithets."

"Oh, didn't that just make our fellows angry?" asked Ned.

"I think not," replied Grandma Elsie. "It seems to have amused them, as they saw that he was ordered down by his superiors."

"Was that a long fight, grandma?" asked Elsie.

"It had lasted thirty-five minutes when the *Boxer* surrendered."

"Had a great many of her men been killed?" asked Ned.

"I don't know," replied his grandma. "But on the *Enterprise,* there was but one besides Burrows. A midshipman named Kerwin Waters, who had been mortally wounded, died a few weeks later. He was buried by the side of his gallant leader — Burrows."

"Oh, dear!" sighed little Elsie. "War is most certainly dreadful!"

"It is, indeed," said her grandma. "And it was made especially dreadful at that time to the people of this country by reason of our being so much weaker than England in men, money, and ships."

"It was a blessing that our seamen were so much more skillful than hers, Grandma Elsie," said Max, who had drawn near in time to hear the last few sentences. "Our little navy did good work in that war, small as she was in comparison with the enemy's. We had twenty ships to her thousand, yet we showed ourselves strong enough to put an end to her tyrannical conduct toward our poor sailors. She has never interfered again in that way."

"And never will, I think," added Grandma Elsie. "The two Anglo-Saxon nations are good friends now, and I trust always will be."

"I hope so, indeed," said Max. "We must be prepared for war, but I hope we may be long able to maintain peace with all other nations."

"A hope in which we can all join, I think," said Mrs. Travilla, glancing around upon the circle of interested faces, for all the *Dolphin's* passengers had by this time gathered about them.

"You were talking of the War of 1812. Were you, mother?" asked Captain Raymond.

"Yes. I was telling the children of the fight between the *Boxer* and the *Enterprise*," replied Mrs. Travilla.

"Oh, won't you tell us some more, grandma?" entreated Ned.

"I think your father could do it better," she said, looking persuasively at the captain.

"I am not sure at all of that," he said. "But if you wish it, I will tell what I can remember of such occurrences at the points along the coast which we are about to visit. But first, let me beg that everyone is free to leave the vicinity should my story seem too dull and prosy," he added with a smiling glance about upon the little company. There was a moment's pause. Then Violet said laughingly, "That was very kind and thoughtful of you, my dear, and I, for one, shall not hesitate to go should I feel inclined."

The captain responded with a bow and smile. Then, after a moment's pause, he began at once upon the chosen theme.

CHAPTER SECOND

"EASTPORT, WHICH WE will presently visit," began Captain Raymond, "is on Moose Island in Passamaquoddy Bay. At the time of our last war with them, the English claimed it as belonging to New Brunswick under the treaty of 1783. Early in July of 1814, Sir Thomas Hardy sailed secretly from Halifax for that place with quite a force of men for land and sea service. On the eleventh, the squadron entered Passamaquoddy Bay and anchored off Fort Sullivan at Eastport. Major Perley Putnam was in command of the fort with a garrison of fifty men and six pieces of artillery. Hardy demanded an instant surrender, and he gave only five minutes' time for consideration. Putnam promptly refused to surrender, but the inhabitants of the island were greatly alarmed and not disposed to resist. So they entreated him to yield, which he did on condition that private property should be respected.

"When the agreement was signed, the British took possession of the fort, the town of Eastport, and all the islands and villages in and around Passamaquoddy Bay, landing a thousand armed men with women and children, fifty or sixty pieces of cannon, and a battalion of artillery."

"And did they stay there, papa?" asked Elsie. "Oh, I hope they are not there now!"

"I have no doubt that nearly, if not all of them, are in their graves by this time, daughter," replied the captain. Then he went on, "The British made declaration that these islands were in their permanent possession, and they ordered all the inhabitants to take an oath of allegiance within seven days or leave the territory."

"Allegiance to the King of England, papa?" asked Elsie. "Did any of them do it?"

"Yes, that is what was meant, daughter, and about two-thirds of the people took it. They, the English, took all the public property from the customs house and tried to force the collector to sign unfinished treasury notes to the value of nine thousand dollars. But he refused, saying, 'Hanging will be no compulsion.'"

"Did that mean that he wouldn't do it even if he knew they would hang him if he refused?" asked Elsie quietly.

"Yes, that was just it," said her father. "Having accomplished what he wished to do at Eastport—securing it to his country, as he thought—leaving eight hundred troops to hold it, Hardy sailed away along the coast of Maine and Massachusetts, spreading alarm as he went. But the people prepared to meet his expected attack—manning their forts and arming them. When Sherbrook and Griffith sailed, they intended to stop at Machais and take possession of it, but falling in with the brig *Rifleman* and being told by its commander that the United States corvette *John Adams* had gone up the Penobscot, they made haste to the mouth of that river to blockade her. They passed up the Green Island channel and entered the fine harbor of Castine on the morning of the first of September. On the edge of the water south of the village was the half moon redoubt called Fort Porter armed with four twenty-pounders and two field pieces and manned by about forty men under Lieutenant Lewis of the United States Army. At sunrise, Lewis was called upon to surrender. He saw that resistance would be impossible, so he resolved to flee. He gave the enemy a volley from his twenty-pounders, then he spiked them, blew up the redoubt, and with the field pieces, he and the garrison fled over the high peninsula to its neck and escaped up the Penobscot. Then the British took possession of the town and control of the bay.

"The *John Adams* had just come home from a successful cruise, and coming into Penobscot Bay in a thick fog, she had struck a rock and received so much injury that it was found necessary to lay her up for repairs. They did their best to take her out of harm's way, but it was with difficulty they could keep her afloat till she reached Hampden, a few miles below Bangor. Some of her crew were also disabled by sickness. So she was almost helpless.

"Sherbrook, the commanding officer of the British vessels, was told all this as soon as he landed at Castine, and he and Griffith, commander of the fleet, at once sent a land and naval force to seize and destroy the *John Adams*. The expedition sailed in the afternoon of the day of the arrival at Castine. The people along the Penobscot were not at all inclined to submit to the British if they could possibly escape doing so. On the day the British sailed up the river, word was sent by express to Captain Morris, and he at once communicated with Brigadier-general John Blake at his home in Brower, opposite Bangor, asking him to call out the militia immediately. Blake lost no time in assembling the tenth Massachusetts division, of which he was the commander. That evening, he rode down to Hampden, where he found Captain Morris busy with his preparations for defense. He had taken the heavy guns of his ship to the high right bank of the Soadabscook, fifty rods from the wharf, and placed them in battery there so as to command the river approaches from below.

"The very next morning, he and Blake held a consultation on the best methods of defense, citizens of Bangor and Hampden taking part in it. Captain Morris had little confidence in the militia, but he expressed his intention to meet the enemy at their landing place, wherever that might be, and also his resolution to destroy the *Adams* rather than allow it to fall into their hands.

"Belfast was taken the next morning by General Gosselin at the head of six-hundred troops. At the same time, another detachment marched up the western side of the Penobscot unmolested and reached Bald Hill Cove at five o'clock in the evening. The troops and eighty marines bivouacked there that night in a drenching rain. During that day, about six hundred raw militia, who had never seen anything more like war than their own annual parade, had gathered at Hampden and been posted by General Blake in an admirable position on the brow of a hill. Lieutenant Lewis and the forty men who had fled from Castine had joined him. The artillery company of Blake's brigade was there also with two brass three-pounders. An iron eighteen-pound cannonade from the *Adams* was placed in battery in the road near the meeting house in charge of Mr. Bent of the artillery. Many of the militia were without weapons or ammunition, but Captain Morris supplied them as far as he could.

"While these arrangements were being made, Captain Morris had mounted nine short eighteen-pounders from the *Adams* upon the high bank over Crosby's wharf and placed them in charge of his first lieutenant assisted by the other two. With the rest of his guns, he took position on the wharf with about two hundred seamen and marines and twenty invalids, who were all ready to defend his crippled ship to the last extremity.

"The next morning, all that region was covered by a dense fog. The different British detachments joined together, and by five o'clock, they were moving on toward Hampden, moving cautiously in the mist with a vanguard of riflemen skirted on the flanks with detachments of sailors and marines with a six-pound cannon, a six and a half inch howitzer, and a rocket apparatus. The British vessels at the same time moved slowly up the river within supporting distance.

"Blake had sent out two flank companies to watch and annoy the approaching foe, and between seven and eight o'clock, they reported them as coming up the hill to attack the Americans. The fog was so thick that they could not be seen, but Blake pointed his eighteen-pounder in that direction, his field pieces also, and he fired away with a good deal of effect, as he learned afterward. But the fog was too thick for him to see at the time. His plan was to reserve his musket firing until the enemy should be near enough to be seriously hurt, but his men, being raw militia and without protection of a breast-work in front, lost courage while standing there awaiting the approach of the enemy. When the enemy came suddenly into view, marching at double-quick and firing volleys in rapid succession, they were panic-stricken, broke ranks, and fled in every direction, leaving Blake and his officers alone. Lieutenant Wadsworth saw it all from the upper battery where he was, and he sent word immediately to Morris, who was on the wharf.

"The flight of the militia had left Morris's rear and flank exposed, and he saw that it would be impossible to defend himself against such a force as was about to attack him. He, therefore, ordered Wadsworth to spike his guns and retreat with his men across the bridge over the Soadabscook, while it was yet open, for the stream was fordable only at low water, and the tide was rising.

"Wadsworth obeyed, his rear gallantly covered by Lieutenant Watson and some marines. At the same time, the guns on the wharf were spiked, the *John Adams* was set on fire, and Morris's men retreated across the Soadabscook, he being the last man to leave the wharf. Before he reached the bridge, the British were on the bank above him, but he dashed across the stream, armpit deep in water, and under a galling fire from their muskets, unhurt, joined his friends on the other side. Blake and his officers and a mere remnant of his command among them—all retreated to Bangor. Morris did not stay there, however, but he soon made his way overland to Portland."

"Did the British harm the people in that town, papa?" asked Elsie.

"They did take possession, and there was no further resistance," replied the captain. "Then they sent some vessels with about five hundred men to Bangor. A mile from the town, they were met by a flag of truce from the magistrates, who asked terms of capitulation. The answer was that private property would be respected. It was about ten o'clock when they reached the town, and Commodore Barrie gave notice that if the people would cheerfully send in the required supplies they should not be harmed in person or property. But he had hardly done so before he gave his sailors to understand that they might plunder as much as they pleased."

"And did they, papa?" asked Elsie.

"Yes," he said. "History tells us that almost every store on the western side of the creek, which there empties into the Penobscot, was robbed of all valuable property. Colonel John, however, did all he could to protect the inhabitants. The British forced the people to surrender all their arms, military stores, and public property of every kind and to report themselves prisoners of war for parole with a promise that they would not take up arms against the British.

"Having robbed the people of property worth twenty-three thousand dollars, destroyed, by burning, fourteen vessels, and stolen six, which they carried away with them, they left Bangor for Hampden, which they treated in the same way. There they desolated the church, tearing up the Bibles and psalm books and demolishing the pulpit and pews. Lossing tells us that the total loss of property at Hampden, exclusive of the cargo of the *Commodore Decatur*, was estimated at forty-four thousand dollars. In a note, he adds that Williamson's *History of Maine* says, 'In the midst of the rapine, a committee waited on Barrie and told him that the people expected at his hands the common safeguards of humanity, if nothing more; to which the brutal officer replied, "I have none for you. My business is to burn, sink, and destroy. Your town is taken by storm, and by the rules of war we ought to both lay your village in ashes and put its inhabitants to the sword. But I will spare your lives, though I don't mean to spare your houses."'"

"Oh, what a cruel wretch!" said Evelyn.

"A perfect savage, I should call him!" exclaimed Lucilla hotly.

"I entirely agree with you ladies," said Mr. Lilburn. "I am sorry to have to own him as a countryman of mine."

"Well, Cousin Ronald," returned Mrs. Travilla pleasantly, "there are plenty of Americans of such character that I should be loath to own them as relatives."

"And there were plenty in the days of our two wars with England, as any one must acknowledge, remembering the lawless bands of marauders called Cowboys and Skinners," said Violet. "They were more detestable than the British themselves—even such as that Barrie, Tarleton, and others too numerous to mention."

"Will they ever come again, papa?" asked Ned.

"I think not, son," replied the captain. "Most, if not all of them, are now dead."

"Yes, it must have been a long, long while ago," remarked the little lad reflectively.

"We are going now to Passamaquoddy Bay, aren't we, papa?" asked Elsie.

"Yes," he said. "I hope to reach there quite early this afternoon."

"And I hope we will see all that Lossing tells about," said Gracie.

"I think you may feel reasonably certain of that," her father responded in his usual kindly, pleasant tones.

"We will pass by Machias on the way to Passamaquoddy Bay. Won't we, father?" asked Gracie in her quiet way.

"Yes," he replied. "We are nearing it now."

"Oh, I remember something about what occurred there in the Revolution, but won't you please tell us the story again?" she exclaimed.

"I will," he said. "We had then an exposed coast many miles in extent and not a single armed vessel to protect it, while Britain was the first naval power of the world. A few of our planters and merchants had been trained in the royal navy, and so had a good many American seamen, to some extent, in helping England with her wars with the French in the twenty years preceding our Revolution. But the wise men who were directing public affairs could see no material for organizing a marine force, so they devoted themselves to the business of raising an army. Immediately after the battle of Lexington, the British began depredations along the New England coast, and soon private vessels were launched by patriot volunteers, who armed them as well as they could and did their best to defend the coast.

"You know, news did not fly as fast in those days as it does now. But when at length the people of Machias heard of the affair at Lexington, it of course, caused great excitement and prompted a desire to defend their country against the foe. There in the harbor of Boston lay an armed British schooner called the *Margaretta*. She had two sloops with her, and the three were busied in getting lumber for the British army in Boston. A party of the young men of the town determined to try to capture her while her officers were at church on shore. They seized one of the sloops, chased the schooner out of the harbor, and after a severe fight, the patriots compelled her to surrender.

"It was the first naval engagement of the Revolution. There were forty Americans commanded by Jeremiah O'Brien, and about twenty of them and as many of the British were killed in the fight. The captain of the cutter was one of the mortally wounded. Soon afterward, O'Brien captured two small English cruisers, making their crews prisoners and carrying them to Watertown, where the Provincial Congress of Massachusetts was in session. That body then took measures to establish a coast marine to intercept English transports bringing supplies for the British troops and gave O'Brien employment in that service with a captain's commission.

"The British force under Sherwood and Griffith, after their raid up the Penobscot, went back to Machias. They landed at Buck's Harbor, which is three miles below the town, and marched against the fort, which the garrison deserted and blew up."

"Are we going to Machias now?" asked Ned.

"No," said his father. "We are nearing Passamaquoddy Bay now. We will spend a little time there, then turn and go back to the Penobscot to visit historical scenes along its course. You perhaps remember that the British went there shortly after having taken Eastport and Fort Sullivan on Moose Island in Passamaquoddy Bay. They were taken on the eleventh of July in 1812. Castine was taken on the first of September of the same year."

"About a year after, came the fight between the *Enterprise* and the *Boxer*, which occurred September 5, 1813," observed Max.

"Yes," said his father with a smile. "Of course, you remember the notable victory vouchsafed us by Providence five days later on Lake Erie?"

"Perry's victory, sir? Yes, indeed! I also remember Macdonough's triumph on Lake Champlain, which was given him on the eleventh of the next September in 1814."

They were now entering the bay, and historical reminiscence gave place to talk of the beauty of the scenery. Captain Raymond, who had been there before, pointed out and named the different islands and villages. They did not land but steamed slowly about the bay, finding so much to interest them that they lingered there until nightfall. They then steamed out into the ocean, taking a westward course. It was a beautiful moonlight evening, and all gathered together on deck, passing the time in cheerful chat concerning the scenes just visited and those they expected to visit in the near future. At length, there was a pause in the conversation, presently broken by little Ned.

"Oh, dear!" he sighed. "I'm just hungry for a little fun. I don't see what's the use of having ventriloquists along if they don't make some fun for us once in a while."

"Now, Master Ned, do you call that polite speech?" asked a strange voice that seemed to come from a short distance in his rear.

Ned sprang to his feet and turned toward it.

"I—I didn't mean to be rude, Cousin Ronald or Brother Max, whichever you are, but I am ever so hungry for a bit of fun."

"And you consider that a healthful appetite, do you?" queried the voice.

"Yes, sir. For 'Laugh and grow fat' is an old saying, so I've heard."

"Well, well, well! I had understood that you rather objected to being considered fat," laughed the invisible speaker.

"Oh, well, I don't believe a bit of fun once in a while would do much harm in that way," returned the little fellow. "At any rate, I'm more than willing to try it."

"Well, suppose we go ahead and try it with the understanding that if you get too fat you are to be reduced to your present suitable size by a low and spare diet?"

"No, indeed!" cried Ned. "I won't consent to that. Don't you know that boys need to eat plenty if they are to grow up into big, strong men?"

"Enough, but not too much, Neddie," laughed his cousin, Dr. Percival, sitting near.

"Uncle Harold, you know all about it, for you're a good doctor," said Ned, appealing to Dr. Travilla. "Oughtn't little boys to have plenty to eat to grow big and strong?"

"Yes, Ned, plenty but not too much."

"Well, that's what I want," laughed Ned. "Oh, what was that?" he started, as a cry of, "Help! Help, or I shall drown!" came from the water not far from the side of the vessel. Cousin Ronald and Max exchanged inquiring glances, and the latter rose hastily to his feet.

"Throw him a rope, my men!" he called to a group of sailors at the farther end of the vessel.

The words had hardly left his lips ere the order was obeyed, and the next moment the dripping figure of a young lad in a bathing suit was drawn up and landed upon the deck.

"Thanks, thanks, gentlemen," he panted. "You've helped me to a narrow escape from a watery grave. I ventured out too far alone in the moonlight and—"

"Don't try to talk, my man. You are too much exhausted," interrupted Dr. Travilla, for he, Captain Raymond, Max, Mr. Lilburn, Chester, and Dr. Percival had all hurried to the spot to see and assist the rescued stranger.

"Thanks! I'll do it," he said. "If you'll kindly help me rub down and lend me some things till these can be made dry."

"Certainly," replied Captain Raymond. At once, he gave directions that the stranger be taken to a comfortably warm stateroom, provided with everything needful, and have his wet garments dried and returned to him as quickly as possible. Then, turning to his brother-in-law, "I leave the rest to your care, Harold," he said.

"Oh, Brother Max," cried Ned, as the group of gentlemen rejoined the ladies and children, "I thought it was you or Cousin Ronald calling for help just for fun, and it was a real drowning man, after all."

"A mere lad, Ned, and I am very glad we were able to give him help in season."

The incident had created a little excitement, and all eagerly awaited Harold's report. He rejoined them in a few minutes, looking so undisturbed that they at once felt that his new patient was in no danger.

"He will be all right presently," he said in answer to their eagerly inquiring looks and questions. "When we heard his cry for help, he had hardly more than just realized his danger. He is somewhat ashamed of his venturesomeness and anxious to get back to his friends without letting them know of the peril he was in."

Turning to Captain Raymond, "He would be very glad and grateful if you would go a little out of your way and land him at the spot where he entered the water. In that way, he will be able to steal up to the house of his friends without arousing their suspicions concerning the danger he was in."

"I think we may do that," the captain said in his kindly tones. "It will probably not delay us more than an hour or so, and we are not hurried for time so that we need decline that request."

Max at once gave the necessary orders; the course of the vessel was changed; and ere long the young stranger was landed at the spot where he had entered the water. Then the *Dolphin* proceeded upon her westward way, and when her passengers awoke in the morning, they were nearing Penobscot Bay.

CHAPTER THIRD

ALL WERE QUITE EAGER to visit the historical places immediately upon their arrival. As they entered the harbor of Castine, Mrs. Travilla remarked that it was quite as picturesque as she had expected from Lossing's description.

"Ah, I entirely agree with you, Cousin Elsie," responded Mr. Lilburn. "It is so bonny a place that I do not wonder why it was so coveted by the enemy."

The whole party presently landed, and a guide was found who promised to conduct them to all the points of historical interest. So, they set out upon their search. They very much admired the situation of the town, and the view from it of the bay with its picturesque islands. They visited old Fort George, which had been built by the British in 1779 in the center of the peninsula and repaired, fraised, and armed by them in 1814. It was only a ruin now, but it was an interesting one because of what it had been in those earlier days. The view from its banks, which were about eighteen feet high, was very interesting. Looking northward from the fort, they could see the entrance to the canal on the right that had been cut by the British across Castine Neck, turning the peninsula into an island. It was about eighty rods long and twelve feet deep, and now it had a bridge across it. Between the promontory and an island, could be seen the mouth of the Penobscot River. On the extreme left, they could see the town of Belfast, thirteen miles distant. Leaving that point, they visited the remains of several other forts built by the British, after which they returned to the yacht for the evening meal and the night's rest.

The *Dolphin* was allowed to remain stationary until all her passengers were on deck again the next morning. Then the anchor was lifted, and she steamed up the river. Favored with delightful weather, they greatly enjoyed the trip up the beautiful, winding stream. They had taken on board a man who was well acquainted with the river and every point of interest upon its banks and who pointed out each one as they neared it. As they entered Marsh Bay, the young people were told that the British squadron lay there one night on their way to Hampton. Elsie and Ned showed keen interest when told of it and in hearing from their father of the cannon ball of the British that lodged in a storehouse there in 1814.

"Do you remember the story that Lossing tells about a Norway pine somewhere in the region?" asked Mrs. Travilla, addressing Captain Raymond.

"Something of it," he said with an amused smile, and the children at once begged to hear it.

"Will you gratify them, mother?" asked the captain. "You probably have a better recollection of his story than I."

"I will do my best," she said and began at once. "Lossing says the tree was about a mile above here. It was the only one of its kind in that region—a round, compact tree, its short trunk looking as if composed of a group of smaller ones and the limbs growing so near the ground that it was difficult to get under it. At the time that the British landed at Frankford, some man who had a quantity of bacon, being afraid they would rob him of it, carried it to that tree and hung the pieces in among the branches to hide them from the foe. Though the British passed along the road only a short distance from the tree, they did not notice its peculiar fruit, so did not meddle with it. His bacon was saved, and always afterward that Norway pine was called the Bacon Tree."

"Thank you, grandma. That was a nice story," said Elsie.

"Don't you have another little story for us, grandma?" asked Ned in coaxing tones. "I do always like your stories ever so much."

At that, Grandma Elsie laughed a pleasant, little laugh and went on, "Lossing tells us quite an interesting little story of a remarkable black man whom he visited somewhere near here. His name was Henry Van Meter, and he was then ninety-five years old. During the Revolution, he was a slave to Governor Nelson of Virginia. After that, he became a seaman and was one of the crew of the privateer *Lawrence*, which sailed from Baltimore in 1814. I suppose Lossing questioned him about his long life and heard his story of it. He remembered having seen Washington many times. The estate of Governor Nelson, his first master, was sold after the war to pay his debts, and Henry was bought by a planter beyond the Blue Ridge. The new master wanted him to marry one of his slave girls and told him if he did, he would order in his will that he should be made a free man at his — the master's — death. In telling of it, Henry said, 'I didn't like the gals, and I didn't want to wait for dead men's shoes. So master sold me to a man near Lexington, Kentucky, and there was only one log house in that town when I went there.'

"He was soon sold to another man, who treated him shamefully. So, one night, he mounted one of his master's horses and fled to the Kentucky River, where he turned the horse loose. He told him to go home if he had a mind to, as he didn't want to steal him. Some kind, white people helped Henry over the river into Ohio, and at Cincinnati, he then took the name of Van Meter — the family name of some of the Shenandoah Valley People who had been kind to him.

"Afterward, Henry became the servant of an officer in the army of General St. Clair and served with our troops in the Northwest under General Wayne. After that, he lived in Chillicothe and then came east to Philadelphia. There, some Quakers paid for him to go school, and he learned to read and write. He became a sailor and went to Europe several times in that capacity. When the war broke out, he shipped as such on board the privateer *Lawrence*. It was taken by the British, and he was thrown into Dartmoor Prison. He witnessed the massacre there in 1815."

"Oh, what was that, grandma?" asked Ned in tones of excitement. "I don't think I have ever heard about that."

"Lossing tell us," replied his grandmother, "that Dartmoor was a depot for prisoners in England. It was situated in a desolate region and was built in 1809 as a place in which to confine French prisoners. At the time the treaty of peace was made with us, there were six thousand American prisoners in it—among them, 2,500 American seamen, who had been put there for refusing to fight in the British navy against their countrymen. They were there when the war began in 1812. For some unknown reason, there was great delay in setting those prisoners free after the treaty of peace was made. It was nearly three months before they even knew that the treaty had been signed. From the time they first heard of it, every day they were expecting to be set at liberty and naturally grew very impatient over the delay. On the fourth of April, they demanded bread instead of hard biscuit, which they refused to eat. On the evening of the sixth, they showed great unwillingness to obey the order to retire to their quarter, and some of them not only refused to do that but went beyond their prescribed limits. Then Captain Shortland, who had charge of the military guard, ordered them to fire on the Americans, which they did. The soldiers, I believe, also fired a second time. Five prisoners were killed, and thirty-three were wounded."

"Why, that was murder. Wasn't it, grandma?" asked Ned. "Didn't they hang those soldiers for doing it?"

"No. The British authorities called it 'justifiable homicide,' which means it was all right enough."

"In which decision I, for one, am far from agreeing," remarked Mr. Lilburn emphatically.

"It created intense indignation in this country at the time," said the captain. "But it is now seldom remembered, and the two nations are, and I hope always will be, good friends."

The *Dolphin* ascended the river only as far as Bangor and returned by moonlight to Castine, where they anchored for some hours. Then, at an early hour in the morning, they steamed out into the ocean again and pursued a westward course until they reached Portland. There they landed and paid a visit to the cemetery where lay the remains of the brave captains of the *Enterprise* and the *Boxer* and those of Midshipman Kerwin Waters.

"They are buried side by side, as if they were brothers instead of enemies who were killed fighting each other," said little Elsie softly. "But perhaps they were good Christian men, each fighting for what he thought was the right of his own country. Papa, can you tell us about the funeral? I suppose they had one?"

"Yes, daughter, a solemn and imposing one. The two battered vessels were lying at the end of Union Wharf. A civil and military procession had been formed at the courthouse at nine in the morning of the ninth of September. The coffins were brought from the vessels in barges of ten oars each and were rowed by minute strokes of ship masters and mates. Most of the barges and boats in the harbor accompanied them. When the barges began to move and while the procession was passing through the streets to the church, minute guns were fired by artillery companies. These same guns were fired while the procession marched from the church to the cemetery here, which is about a mile distant from the church.

"The chief mourners who followed the corpse of Captain Burrows were Dr. Washington, Captain Hull, and officers of the *Enterprise*. Those who followed Captain Blyth's were the officers of the *Boxer*, who were allowed a parole. Both were followed by naval and military officers in the United States service, the crews of the two vessels, civil officers of the state and city, military companies, and a large concourse of citizens. Only a few weeks before, Captain Blyth was one of the pall-bearers at the funeral of our Lawrence, the gallant commander of the *Chesapeake* at Halifax."

"That dear brave man that said, 'Don't give up the ship,' papa?" asked Elsie.

"Yes, daughter. Now, let us read the inscription on his tombstone: 'In memory of Captain Samuel Blyth, late Commander of his Britannic Majesty's brig *Boxer.* He nobly fell on the fifth day of September, 1813, in action with the United States brig *Enterprise.* In life honorable; in death glorious. His country will long deplore one of her bravest sons, his friends long lament one of the best of men. AE. 29. The surviving officers offer this feeble tribute of admiration and respect.'"

"It sound as though they had respected and loved him," said the little girl. "That next grave is where Burroughs lies. Isn't it, papa? Won't you please read its inscription?"

They drew nearer, and the captain read aloud: "'Beneath this stone moulders the body of William Burrows, late commander of the United States brig *Enterprise,* who was mortally wounded on the fifth of September, 1813, in an action which contributed to increase the fame of American valor, by capturing his Britannic Majesty's brig *Boxer,* after a severe contest of forty-five minutes. AE. 28. A passing stranger has erected this memento of respect to the manes of a patriot, who, in the hour of peril, obeyed the loud summons of an injured country, and who gallantly met, fought, and conquered foeman.'"

"And that one on the pillars, papa, whose is it?" Elsie asked, as her father paused in his recital with a slight sigh.

"That is the tomb of Midshipman Waters," he said. "We will go nearer and read its inscription: 'Beneath this marble, by the side of his gallant commander, rest the remains of Lieutenant Kerwin Waters, a native of Georgetown, District of Columbia, who received a mortal wound, September 5, 1813, while a midshipman on board the United States brig *Enterprise,* in action with his Britannic Majesty's brig *Boxer,* which terminated in the capture of the latter. He languished in severe pain, which he endured with fortitude, until September 25, 1813, when he died with Christian calmness and resignation, aged eighteen. The young men of Portland erect this stone as a testimony of their respect for his valor and virtues.'"

"Twenty days to suffer so," sighed Elsie. "Oh, it must have been dreadful!"

Max and Evelyn stood near, side by side.

"Dreadful indeed!" Evelyn sighed in low and quivering tones as they turned away. "Oh, Max! I wish you did not belong to the navy!"

"Why, dearest?" he asked in tender tones. "It is not only in the navy that men die suddenly and of injuries. Many a naval officer has lived to old age and died at home in his bed. And we are under the same Protecting Care on the sea as on the land, dearest."

"Yes, that is a cheering thought," she said. "And since you love the sea, it is wrong and selfish of me to regret your choice of a profession. And I could not be induced to resign my sailor lover for any landsman," she added with a charming blush and smile.

✄ ✄ ✄ ✄ ✄

That evening, joining her father as she so often did in his quiet promenade of the deck of the *Dolphin* before retiring for the night, Lucilla spoke of their visit to the cemetery and said, "I have always been so glad that you left the navy, papa, so that we could have you always at home with us. I am gladder still, when I think that if we should have another war you will not be in danger of such a fate as that which befell Burrows and Blyth."

"Unless I am needed, volunteer my services, and am accepted," he quickly returned in a slightly playful tone.

"Oh, papa, don't. Please don't!" she exclaimed, clinging more closely to him. "It would be dreadful enough to have Max in such danger but to have you, too, in it would be heart-breaking."

"Well, dear child, we won't be so foolish as to trouble ourselves about what may never happen. And if it ever should happen, we must put our trust in the Lord, believing that He doeth all things well and trusting His promise, 'As thy days are, so shall thy strength be.' And you can rejoice in the fact that Chester is neither sailor nor soldier," he added with a smile, softly patting the head resting upon his arm.

"Yes, father dear, that is no small comfort," she said, "especially as I know he is patriotic enough to do all in his power for his country."

"Ah, no doubt of that! I think Chester would be as ready as any one else to take up arms in her defense if he saw that his services were needed. And I don't believe this daughter of mine would say a word to prevent him."

"I think not, papa, but I hope I may never be tried in that way."

"A hope in which I heartily join you, daughter. I should be glad, indeed, to know that we were done with wars. But that is so uncertain that we, as a nation, must be ever prepared to repel attack on land or sea. 'Eternal vigilance is the price of liberty.'"

"And liberty is well worth that price, isn't it, father?" she said with a bright smile up into his face.

"Yes. So we think. We could never be content without it."

They paced silently back and forth for a few moments, and then Lucilla asked, "How long are we going to lie quietly here in the harbor at Portland, papa?"

"That will depend upon the wishes of the majority of our company," he answered, "which I think we can learn at the breakfast table tomorrow morning."

CHAPTER FOURTH

IT WAS A BRIGHT and cheerful party that gathered about the *Dolphin's* breakfast table the next morning. Greetings were exchanged, a blessing asked upon the food, and Captain Raymond began helping his guests.

"I notice we are still lying quietly in Portland harbor," remarked Dr. Percival. "Do we remain here another day, captain?"

"That must be as the majority decide," was the pleasant-toned rejoinder. "Please, friends, express your wishes freely."

No one spoke for a moment—each waiting for the others. Then Violet said in her lively, pleasant way, "Cousin Ronald, you are the eldest, and you should feel entitled to speak first."

"Thanks, cousin," he returned, "but I really have no choice. I am perfectly willing to go or stay, as may best please the majority of my friends here."

"Do you think of returning directly to Bar Harbor, captain?" asked Mrs. Travilla.

"If that is what you would all prefer, mother. But how would you all like to take a short sea voyage—sailing directly eastward from here, at some distance from the coast, and perhaps going up the coast of New Brunswick?"

Every one, from Mr. Lilburn down to little Ned, seemed charmed with the idea, and as the weather was all that could be desired, it was decided that they would start as soon as the anchor could be lifted and sufficient steam gotten up. They carried out their plan, and they all had a delightful voyage lasting several days.

It was on Saturday that they left Portland. The Sabbath found them far from land, and, as at former times, services were conducted on board the yacht with the singing of hymns, the offering up of prayers, the reading of the scriptures, and of a sermon by Captain Raymond.

After that, they formed themselves into a Bible class, and Mr. Lilburn was persuaded to take the lead, choosing the subject while the others sat about him, Bibles in hand. Opening his, the dear old gentleman began, "Let us take for our theme Jesus Christ our Lord, and what it is so to know Him that we shall have eternal life. Here in the seventeenth chapter of John's gospel in His — the Master's — wonderful prayer we read: 'And this is life eternal, that they might know Thee the only true God, and Jesus Christ, whom Thou hast sent.' Paul tells us in his letter to the Philippians, 'I count all things but loss for the excellency of the knowledge of Jesus Christ my Lord.' His acquaintance was not with the Christ of Galilee, whom he had not known, but with the ascended Christ — He who said to the Apostle John on Patmos, 'I am

He that liveth and was dead, and behold I am alive again forever more.' In the tenth verse of the first chapter of his gospel, John tells us: 'He was in the world and the world was made by Him and the world knew Him not.' In First John third chapter and last clause of the first verse: 'Therefore the world knoweth us not, because it knew Him not.' A self-seeking and worldly-minded man does not know Christ, and this man cannot understand a man who is aiming day by day to live above the world and get the Christ-view of life. Captain, can you tell us why it is that the worldly-minded do not know Jesus?"

"Because," replied the captain, "the cares and pleasures of this world are crowding Him out of their hearts, as He Himself tells us in the parable of the sower. But some of those who loved Him failed for a time to recognize Him when He was close to them. In the last chapter of his gospel, John tells us: 'But when the morning was now come, Jesus stood on the shore; but the disciples knew not that it was Jesus.' Mary also had failed at first to recognize Him when He spoke to her as she stood weeping beside His sepulchre. And how long He talked with those two on the way to Emmaus, and they did not recognize Him until He sat down to eat with them, took bread, blessed, and brake it. Then He vanished out of their sight! Ah, Jesus is often near us, and we know Him not."

"And He is our Master," said Mrs. Travilla in her low, sweet tones. "In John thirteen, thirteenth verse, talking with His disciples, Jesus says: 'Ye call me Master and Lord; and ye say well, for so I am.' And Paul tells the Ephesians that their Master is in heaven. 'And ye masters do the same things unto them, forbearing, threatening, knowing that your Master also is in heaven.'"

"There are five Greek words translated Master," commented the captain. "One means overseer; another teacher; still another signifying absolute ownership; another, leader—one who goes before us; still another, one exercising supreme authority or power. Oh, that today each one of us may know Christ as our supreme Lord and Master who alone has absolute ownership of our lives and all of our powers."

"Let us look for other texts bearing upon this subject," said Mr. Lilburn. "Have not you one for us, Harold?"

"Yes," replied Harold, "here in First John and the second chapter is given a test of our knowledge of Christ. 'Hereby do we know that we know Him if we keep His commandments. He that saith I know Him and keepeth not His commandments is a liar and the truth is not in him.'"

"And here in John's gospel," said Mrs. Lilburn, "where Jesus is talking with his disciples that same night in which he was betrayed. He says: 'A new commandment I give unto you, That ye love one another; as I have loved you, that ye also love one another. By this shall men know that ye are my disciples, if ye have love one to another.'"

"And again," said Evelyn, "in the fifteenth chapter and twelfth verse, 'This is my commandment, that ye love one another, as I have loved you. Greater love hath no man than this, that a man lay down his life for his friends.'"

"What wonderful love—oh, what wonderful love—was His!" exclaimed Mrs. Travilla in low, moved tones. "And how sweet are those words: 'I have loved thee with an everlasting love.' 'For a small moment have I forsaken thee; but with great mercies will I gather thee.'"

"Let us sing His praise," suggested Mr. Lilburn, and Violet, seating herself at the instrument, struck a few chords and started the hymn:

Oh, for a thousand tongues to sing,
My great Redeemer's praise . . .

the others joining in with a will, all evidently singing with spirit and understanding, for the sweet words were familiar to all.

🙙 🙙 🙙 🙙 🙙

For a few moments afterward, Mrs. Travilla and her cousin and long-time friend Annis—now Mrs. Lilburn—were together a little apart from the others, talking low and confidentially. They talked of the past, the present, and the future, as regarded life in both this world and the next.

"How sweet is that Bible lesson that we have just had," said Annis at length. "How I love those words of Jesus: 'Ye call me Master and Lord; and ye say well; for so I am.'"

"Yes," returned Elsie, "they are very dear to me. Oh, how sweet to know that He is ever with us — always close at hand, full of love, infinite in power and willingness to bless and to help in every trouble. He is always willing to give 'the oil of joy for mourning and the garment of praise for the spirit of heaviness.' Oh, how true are the words: 'The joy of the Lord is your strength.' Even if we only have that, we can bear all troubles and trials. It makes one happy in the present and takes away all dread of the future. So sweet and sustaining is it to know that He who has all power in heaven and earth is your friend, loving you with an everlasting, infinite love and caring for you at all times and in all places."

"Yes, yes, yes," said Annis softly. "'Sing, O daughter of Zion; shout, O Israel; be glad and rejoice with all your heart, O daughter of Jerusalem.' 'The Lord thy God in the midst of thee is mighty; He will save, He will rejoice over thee with joy; He will rest in His love, He will joy over thee with singing.' Are they not such sweet words, Elsie?"

"Indeed they are, Annis! These others, too. 'God commendeth His love toward us, in that while we were yet sinners, Christ died for us.'"

There was a moment of silence. Then Annis said, "You seem to me a very happy Christian, Elsie. Is it not because the joy of the Lord is indeed your strength?"

"Oh, Annis, who could be otherwise than happy in the consciousness of that love and in the thought of how soon one will be with the Master and like Him and with all the dear ones who have gone before—never, ever to again be separated from them?"

"Yes, dear cousin, and how blest are we in the knowledge that our dear ones gone before were His, are with Him now, and will be ready to greet us with great joy when we, too, shall reach that blessed shore."

"'The joy of the Lord is our strength,'" again quoted Mrs. Travilla in her low, sweet tones. "Don't you think, Annis, that some of the Covenanters and the Puritans—good, devoted Christians as most of them were—in opposing the lightness, worldly-mindedness, and frivolity of their foes, may have gone too far to the other extreme, leaving out from their teachings the joy of the Lord? Do you not remember that the Jews were told by Nehemiah, Ezra, and the others, 'This day is holy unto the Lord your God; mourn not nor weep. Go your way, eat the fat and drink the sweet; and send portions unto them for whom nothing is prepared; for this day is holy unto our Lord; neither be ye sorry; for the joy of the Lord is your strength. So the Levites stilled all people, saying, "Hold your peace, for the day is holy; neither be ye grieved." And all the people went their way, to eat, and to drink, and to send portions, and to make great mirth, because they had understood the words that were declared unto them.'"

"Yes," said Annis, "it seems to be human nature to go to extremes, and I think much harm is often done in that way. For instance, the Covenanters and Puritans of old times were so disgusted with the errors and selfish indulgences of the church of their time—turning the Sabbath into a holiday, which might rightly be spent in merrymaking and sport—that they themselves robbed it of all enjoyment and made it a dull, gloomy time to their young people with little or no hint in it of the strengthening joy of the Lord."

"I think you are right," returned Mrs. Travilla in a musing tone. "The Sabbath is not a day for frivolity, but it is one for joy and gladness—the joy of the Lord strengthening us for duty, trial, and temptation. What but that sustained the martyrs when called upon to lay down their lives for the sake of Him who died to redeem them? And oh, how that gracious, precious promise, 'As thy days, so shall thy strength be,' relieves one of the dread of what the future may have in store for us—bereavements, losses, or sufferings, mental or physical! How often and sweetly He bids us fear not. 'O Israel, Fear not: for I have redeemed thee, I have called thee by thy name; thou art mine. When thou passest through the waters, I will be with thee; and through the rivers, they shall not overflow thee: when thou walkest through the fire, thou shalt not be burned; neither shall the flames kindle upon thee. For I am the Lord, thy God, the Holy One of Israel, thy Savior.'"

"Yes," said Annis, "oh, how very often, how tenderly he bids us fear not. It is like a mother hushing her frightened child. 'Say to them that are of a fearful heart, fear not . . . Fear thou not for I am with thee . . . For I the Lord thy God will hold thy right hand, saying to thee, fear not, I will help thee. Fear not, O Jacob my servant, and Jerusalem whom I have chosen.'"

"'Whom I have chosen,'" repeated Elsie. "How those words bring to mind what Jesus our dear Master said to His disciples in that last talk with them in the room where they had eaten the passover: 'Ye have not chosen Me, but I have chosen you.' Oh, what love and condescension to choose us sinful creatures for His own!"

"'And ordained you that ye should go and bring forth fruit,'" said Annis, going on with the quotation, "'and that your fruit should remain; that whatsoever ye shall ask the Father in My name, He will give it you.' I remember," she went on musingly, "that when I was a little girl I used to think I should like to be a Christian and would be if only I knew how. The way seems very easy now—just to listen to the dear Saviour's gracious invitation, 'Come unto me all ye that labor and are heavy laden, and I will give you rest.' All one need do is accept it and give themselves to Him."

"Yes," said Elsie. "His promise joined to that—'and ye shall find rest unto your souls'—is sure. It never fails."

CHAPTER FIFTH

BEFORE THE NEXT Sabbath the travelers had returned to Bar Harbor. For some weeks longer they remained in that vicinity. Then, cooler weather making a more southerly climate desirable, they sailed for home. Dr. Percival was so far recovered that he felt in haste to get back to Torriswood and at work among his patients again. He and his Maud paid a flying visit to old friends and relatives at Roselands, the Oaks, and Ion, and then they hastened to Louisiana by rail.

Max Raymond, to the great satisfaction of his fiancée and his friends, was favored with a lengthening of his furlough, which enabled him to spend some weeks at home in his father's house. Lucilla persuaded Evelyn to be her guest at the same time. Chester was there every evening, and so courting went merrily on. There was much talk about the new house the captain proposed building and much discussion of the question whether the one building should be made suitable and sufficiently large for two families—half of it for Max and Eva—or whether a separate house should be put up for them in another part of the grounds. The decision was finally left to the brides-elect. As they were very strongly attached, and Max was likely to be often away at sea for months and years together, they thought it best the two dwellings should be under one roof. Their decision was highly approved by the captain and all their relatives and friends.

Then followed consultations in regard to the exact spot upon which it should stand, and the studying and comparing of plans to make it as commodious, convenient, and beautiful as possible. The captain was evidently ready to go to any reasonable amount of expense in order to give them an ideal home, his means being ample and his love for his children very great.

But all the time was not spent in that way, for other relatives claimed a share in Max's prized companionship. Invitations were given, and visits were paid to the Oaks, Ion, Fairview, the Laurels, Roselands, Pinegrove, Ashlands, and Riverside. Sometimes the invitation was for dinner or tea—sometimes for the whole day or longer for the young folks, if not for the older ones and their children. It was on the last day of October they dined at Riverside, nearly all the connection meeting them there. At Rosie's earnest solicitation, Evelyn and Lucilla, Max and Chester accepted an invitation to stay until the next morning, Captain Raymond giving a rather unwilling consent to let Lucilla do so.

"It's Hallowe'en, you know, and I am simply pining for a bit of fun," Rosie said privately to the girls after seeing the older guests depart. "You two are engaged, to be sure, but 'there's many a slip 'twixt the cup and the lip,'" she added with a laugh and a twinkle of fun in her eye.

"We are not wanting slips," laughed Lucilla.

"Nor much afraid we will get them," added Evelyn merrily. "Still we might have a little fun."

"Provided we take it early enough to get to bed in good season," added Lucilla in a mirthful tone. "My father, as you know, is very particular about that—so kindly anxious is he to keep me in good health."

"Which is altogether right, wise, and kind, I am sure," returned Rosie. "I don't intend to tempt you to go contrary to his wishes. I'm obliged to him for granting my request for permission to keep you here all night, and I shall not urge you to stay up later than he would allow you if you were at home. If we try some old-fashioned games, we can suit ourselves as to the hour for the experiments."

"Yes," laughed Evelyn, "I shall be quite as sure of the fulfillment of the augury if we get it some hours earlier than people of old times used to look for it."

"Then we will just wait till our folks get to bed, which they always do in good season," said Rosie.

"Your husband heartily approves, I suppose?" remarked Lucilla inquiringly.

"Oh, yes!" laughed Rosie. "He sees no harm in it and approves of his wife having all the pleasure she can. I wish we could have had Gracie stay and share the fun, but her father vetoed that almost before I had fairly given the invitation."

"Yes," said Lucilla, "poor Gracie is so feeble that father has to be very careful of her."

"Yes. I know, but I thought he might have left her for once, considering that my two doctor brothers are here for the night as well unless called out by some inconveniently sick person," said Rosie.

"Which we will hope they won't be, for even doctors should have a little amusement once in a while," said Evelyn.

"Yes," said Rosie, "and they enjoyed the golf this afternoon and appear to be having a pleasant time with Max, Chester, and the others out on the river bank there now."

The girls were on the veranda overlooking the river, and just at that moment they were joined by Rosie's mother-in-law, the older Mrs. Croly. She sat down and chatted with them for a few moments, then bade them goodnight, and went to her own apartments. It was growing dusk then, the young men came in, and presently they all repaired to the drawing room, where for the next hour or two they entertained each other with music and conversation. Max had some interesting adventures to narrate, to which both young men and maidens were eager listeners.

In the pause that followed the conclusion of the second tale, the clock in the hall tolled.

"Eleven!" exclaimed Lucilla in a tone of great surprise and dismay. "Father would say I ought to have gone to my room and my bed more than an hour ago."

"Oh, no! Not on Hallowe'en," laughed Rosie. Just then a servant brought in a basket filled with ears of corn and set it down in their midst.

"What's that for, Rosie?" asked Harold. "You can hardly ask your guests to eat raw corn, especially at this late hour? As a physician I must most emphatically enter my protest."

"Perhaps Rosie is benevolently trying to bring practice into her brothers' hands," remarked Herbert facetiously. "But we are not looking for that at present but for fun that will hurt no one."

"Yes, my dear brothers, that's what I am endeavoring to do," she returned in sprightly tones. "Perhaps you have not heard of the new game with ears of corn? You folks are invited to be blindfolded, each in turn, and in that condition draw out an ear of corn by which to foretell your future fate. A tasseled ear will promise you great joy and a big, full one good luck for a year. A short one will mean a gift is coming and a red or yellow one no luck at all."

"Quite a new idea," said Herbert, "and as there is nothing said about love or marriage, I suppose engaged folks may try it—married ones also."

"Oh, yes!" replied Rosie, producing a dainty lace-trimmed handkerchief. "Eva, will you kindly consent to take the first turn?"

"If you wish," returned Evelyn. Then the handkerchief was bound about her head and she was led to the basket.

"I suppose I am not to choose by feeling, either, but just to take the first one I happen to touch?" she said inquiringly.

The others assented, and she drew out an ear.

"Oh, good luck for you!" exclaimed Rosie. "It is as big and full a one as the basket holds."

Lucilla was then told it was her turn, and the handkerchief was bound about her eyes. She stooped over the basket and drew out quite a short ear.

"Ah, you see I am not so lucky as you were, Eva," she exclaimed, passing her fingers from end to end.

"But it isn't bad," said Rosie. "That means a gift is coming to you soon."

"A good or a bad one?" laughed Lucilla. "Perhaps papa would say I deserved a bad one for staying up so late."

"Oh, no! I think he expected something of this kind, which may be why he declined to let Gracie stay," said Rosie. "And I did want her to stay badly. Well, gentlemen, which of you will take his turn now?"

At that, they all insisted that she should take hers first, which she did, bringing out a finely tasseled ear.

"Oh, I am fortunate!" she cried with a merry peal of laughter, "A tasseled ear is said to mean great joy."

After that, the young men took their turns. Chester got a big, full ear; Max got a short one; Herbert got a tasseled one, and Harold a yellow one, which Rosie told him with sighs and groans meant no luck at all.

"But don't be discouraged, brother dear," she said, patting him affectionately on the shoulder. "Though older than myself, you are young enough to have lots of good luck after this year is out."

"Many thanks for the assurance, sister mine," he laughed. "Though older than yourself, I believe I am young enough to wait a year for any special good luck."

"And I hope you will have enough afterward to reward you for the patient waiting, Uncle Harold," said Lucilla.

"If he gets all he deserves, it will be a great deal," added Evelyn.

"You are good, kind comforters — both. Please accept my warmest thanks," laughed Harold.

There was a little more lively chat. Then the young girls said goodnight and went to their rooms — two on the second floor with a communicating door between. Rosie accompanied them, leaving her husband to attend to their gentlemen guests and their needs.

"See here, girls," she said, pointing to a basket of rosy-cheeked apples on a stand. "These were put here to induce you to try another Hallowe'en experiment. If you want to see what your future husbands will look like, eat one of these standing before the mirror, brushing your hair all the time, and now and then — when you can get up courage enough — look over your left shoulder."

"Oh, that won't require any courage, Rosie," laughed Evelyn. "I am not in the least afraid of Max—brave officer though he is."

"And I stand in quite as little fear of Chester," said Lucilla. "So that really it seems that your good apples will be almost thrown away."

"Ah, you two forget the 'many a slip 'twixt the cup and the lip,'" laughed Rosie. "And it cannot possibly do your lovers any harm, or alienate their affections from you."

"No, we are not at all afraid of that," said Lucilla. "As your apples look very tempting, I believe I shall run the risk of eating one presently. I suppose I must first don a dressing gown and take down my hair."

"Yes," said Rosie. "You are to stand before the mirror brushing diligently while eating the apple. And you will try it, too. Won't you, Eva?"

"Well, yes," returned Evelyn, "just for fun, and if anybody but Max comes to me I shall be sure it is not a truthful augury."

"Max is a fine fellow and has always been one of my favorites," said Rosie, "but there are others in the world that might do just as well, in case you and Max should have a falling out. Or you may live long enough to marry several times."

Evelyn laughed at that, saying she was quite sure one would be enough for her.

"I know you girls did not come prepared to stay all night," said Rosie. "So I have laid out a nightdress and dressing gown for each of you. Get into them, and you will both look nice and pretty enough for an interview with your future husbands."

They thanked her, and, examining the garments that she took from a wardrobe in Eva's room, they pronounced them pretty enough to wear to the breakfast table.

They made haste with their preparations, and in a few minutes each was standing before a mirror, eating an apple and brushing out her hair. Rosie left them with a promise to be back again before long to learn of their success. She artfully left ajar both doors leading into the hall. They opened noiselessly, and presently each had admitted a young man, who, wearing slippers, moved with noiseless tread. As the girls looked over their left shoulders, Eva caught sight of Harold standing a few feet in her rear, gazing steadily at her, a kindly smile upon his features. While at the same moment, Lucilla perceived Herbert at a similar distance from her, gazing intently and admiringly upon her.

"Oh, Uncle Herbert," she laughed, "this cannot be a true sign, for I know well enough that neither of us has any loverlike feeling toward the other."

Almost before she finished her sentence, he had vanished, and she heard Evelyn saying in mirthful tones, "Ah, Uncle Harold, this is the 'no luck at all' prophesied by that yellow ear of corn. For, as you well know, I am already pledged to another."

At that Harold sighed deeply and withdrew.

Scarcely had he and his brother disappeared when Max silently took his place, Chester at the same time coming up behind Lucilla so that she saw him in the mirror, to which she had again turned, brush in hand.

"Oh, is it you, Chester? You are the right man in the right place," she laughed.

"I hope so, darling," he returned. "What lovely hair!" passing his hand caressingly over it. "It is so long and thick, too. I never before saw it to such advantage."

Max was standing silently behind Evelyn, and just at that moment, she caught sight of him in the glass. She turned quickly, and he caught her in his arms, giving her a rapturous kiss.

"Don't be disappointed that I am your future mate," he said.

"Certainly not, since you were already my own free choice," she returned, looking up into his face with one of her sweetest smiles. Just then Lucilla's voice was heard coming from the next room, "Is that you, Max?" and in a moment the four were together, merrily laughing and chatting, both young men insisting that that style of wearing their hair—streaming over the shoulders—was extremely becoming. Then Rosie and Will joined them for a moment, after which they all bade goodnight, and the girls were left alone to seek repose.

CHAPTER SIXTH

THE YOUNG PEOPLE had a merry time over their breakfast the next morning, rehearsing all they had gone through in their celebration of Hallowe'en. Each one seemed to have enjoyed his or her part in it. They lingered over the meal, but soon after leaving the table, they scattered to their homes, excepting Eva, who returned to Woodburn with Max and Lucilla.

On arriving there, Lucilla hastened to the library, where she found her father examining some business letters.

"Good morning, papa!" she said. "Here is your amanuensis, and haven't you something for her to do?"

"Yes," he replied, looking up at her with a smile, as she stood close at his side. "The first thing is to give her father a kiss. That is, if she will not find it a disagreeable task."

"Anything other than that, father dear," she returned, bending down to give and receive a caress. "And won't you let me help, as usual, with your correspondence?"

"I shall be very glad to do so," he returned, rising to take the cover from her typewriter and put the paper in place. Then she seated herself, and he began dictating. When they had finished, she asked, "Did you miss me last night and this morning, father?"

"I did indeed," he said. "But, I suppose that is something I will have to get used to, when Chester takes you away from me."

He ended with a sigh.

"Oh, papa, please don't sigh so over it!" she exclaimed. "You know it isn't as if I had to go away a distance from you. I shall be close at hand, and you can call me to your side whenever you will."

"Which will be pretty often, I think," he said with a smile, drawing her closer to him and caressing her hair and cheek with his hand. "Had you a pleasant time last evening? And did you go to bed in season, as your father would have seen that you did had you been at home?"

"No, I did not get to bed early, papa," she replied. "I thought you would excuse me for staying up, for once, to try my fortune. For you see, we all wanted to know who were to be our future life partners. Rosie told us that there was 'many a slip 'twixt the cup and the lips,' so that our engagements didn't make us safe."

She concluded with a light laugh and look that seemed to say she felt no fear that he would be seriously displeased with her.

"You stayed up to try your fortune, did you?" he returned with a look of amusement. "Why, my child, I thought you considered it made."

"So I do, papa, and last night's experience only confirmed my belief."

Then she went on to tell him the whole story, he seeming to enjoy the tale as she told it.

"You are not vexed with me, papa, for staying up so late, just for once?" she asked when her tale was told.

"No," he replied, "though I should be far from willing to have you make a practice of it. For you know, 'Early to bed and early to rise, makes a man healthy, wealthy, and wise,' or so the old saying is, and I want you to be all three."

"As you are, father. I am certainly the first, at all events," she returned with a happy little laugh. "You have never had to pay a big doctor's bill for me."

"No, to escape that is the least of my reasons for wanting to keep you healthy."

Just then Max came in with Eva, bringing a book on architecture.

"Here are some plans for houses, father," he said, laying the book open before the captain. "Please look at this and tell me what you think of it, as in some respects it is what would suit us. You too, Lu. Eva and I like the most of it very much."

The captain and Lucilla examined it with interest and were as well pleased as were Max and Evelyn. It was a matter in which they and Chester also were deeply interested, and they were taking time and trouble to make sure of having their future home all that could be desired. It was not to be built in haste. They had agreed to take plenty of time and thought in regard to all the interior arrangements, making everything as convenient as possible, as well as to the exterior, which they were resolved should be such as to cause the building to be recognized as an ornament to its neighborhood.

Chester was the one most anxious to get the house built and to secure his bride. The other three who were betrothed seemed well content to defer their marriage until the captain should give full and hearty consent.

The exact spot on which the building should stand had been selected, and the plans for it almost matured when there came an order for Max to join a naval vessel about to sail for a distant foreign port.

There was quite a tender and very sorrowful leave-taking, and Max was absent from the home circle for many months.

For a time, those left behind seemed to have lost interest in the building of the new home. Then came the fall rains, after that the winter storms, and it was decided that the actual work should not be begun until spring. Then Gracie had a serious illness, which kept her in bed for several weeks, and she had hardly recovered when the little ones at Fairview were taken down with the measles. They all passed through that trouble safely, but the weather had now grown warm enough to make a more northern climate desirable. They, the whole Fairview family, accompanied by Grandma Elsie and the Raymond family went aboard the captain's yacht and sailed up the coast and the Hudson River to Evelyn's pretty home, Crag Cottage.

That became their headquarters for the summer, though occasional short trips were taken to one or another of the points of interest in New York and the adjoining states. They all enjoyed themselves, though Chester and Max were missed—especially by Lucilla and Evelyn. Chester, however, joined the party late in the season and was with them on the journey home.

Soon after their return, work was begun on the proposed site of the new double dwelling. The cellars were dug, and the foundation was laid. But the work proceeded slowly. Max was not likely to be at home again soon, and it was well to take time to have everything done in the best possible manner.

Evelyn and Lucilla had fully decided upon a double wedding, which could not take place until Max obtained a furlough and came home for a visit of some weeks or months. Chester felt the delay hard upon him, but he had to content himself with being allowed to spend all his spare time with his betrothed.

Fall and winter passed quietly. There were the usual holiday festivities and exchange of gifts with quiet home duties and pleasures filling up the days, and the weeks glided swiftly by.

One morning in February, the captain, looking over his daily paper, uttered an exclamation of mingled regret and indignation.

"What is it, my dear?" asked Violet. "Something that troubles you, I perceive."

"Yes," he replied. "Here is a piece of very bad news. The *Maine*, one of our favorite battleships, lying at anchor in Havana harbor, has been suddenly destroyed by a terrible explosion. She is wrecked and sent to the bottom with 266 American seamen. Only the captain and a few of his officers who were on shore escaped the awful fate of the others."

"Oh, that is dreadful, dreadful!" cried Violet. "But how did it happen? What was the cause?"

"That has yet to be discovered, my dear," replied Captain Raymond. "But I have little doubt that it was the work of some enemy among the Spaniards. They have been angry at the presence of the vessel in their harbor. Their newspapers have called it a taunt and a banter, for they know our people sympathize with the Cubans. Somebody has done this evil deed. It remains to be discovered who it was."

"This is Sigsbee's dispatch to the government," he added and read aloud:

"'*Maine* blown up in Havana Harbor at nine-forty tonight. Many wounded and doubtless more killed or drowned. Wounded and others on board Spanish man-of-war and Ward line steamers. Send lighthouse tenders from Key West for crew and the few pieces of equipment above water.

None has clothing other than that upon him. Public opinion should be suspended until further report. All officers believed to be saved. Jenkins and Merritt not yet accounted for. Many Spanish officers, including representatives of General Blanco, now with me to express sympathy.

—SIGSBEE'"

It was directly after breakfast, and the family were all present. Lucilla and Gracie seemed much excited, and little Ned asked anxiously if "Brother Max" was on that ship.

"No, my son," replied his father. "I am very glad to know certainly that he was not. Have you forgotten that he is with Commodore Dewey on the coast of China?"

"Oh, yes, papa! I forgot where Havana was. I remember now that it is not in China but in Cuba."

"Oh, that is a very dreadful piece of news, papa!" said Lucilla in tones of excitement. "Won't it be likely to bring on a war with Spain—especially as we have been feeling so sorry for the poor Cubans whom she has been abusing so terribly?"

"I am really afraid it can hardly fail to cause war," replied the captain. "But that will depend very much upon the result of the investigation, which will no doubt be promptly made by our own government."

"Oh, I hope we won't have war!" cried Gracie, shuddering at the thought.

"War is a very dreadful thing," sighed her father, "but sometimes the right thing for those who undertake it simply for the sake of the downtrodden and oppressed."

"But we are not such folks. Are we, papa?" asked Ned.

"No, son, but the poor Cubans are. And the question is whether we should not undertake to win their freedom for them."

"By fighting the Spaniards who abuse them so, papa?" asked little Elsie.

"Yes."

"What have they been doing to them, papa?" asked Ned.

"Oppressing, robbing, murdering them, burning down their houses, forcing them into the cities and towns, and leaving them to starve to death there."

"Why, papa, how dreadful! I should think our folks ought to go and fight for them. I wish I was big enough to help."

"My dear little son, I am glad you are not," said his mother, drawing him to her side and giving him a fond caress.

"Why, mamma?"

"Because you might be badly hurt or even killed. That would break your mother's heart."

"Then, mamma, I'm glad I don't have to go, for I wouldn't like to hurt you so," said the little fellow, stroking his mother's cheek and gazing fondly into her eyes.

"Oh, I hope it won't come to war for us!" exclaimed Gracie. "Though I should like to have the poor Cubans helped. Just think how dreadful if Max should be engaged in a naval battle."

"Well, my child, we won't borrow trouble about that," said her father soothingly.

"And I hope there is not much danger, as he is away off in the China seas," said Lucilla, trying to cheer Gracie, though she herself had little idea that he would escape taking part if there should be a war.

"In case of war, that will hardly excuse him from doing his duty," said their father. "Nor would our dear brave boy wish to be excused. But we will all pray that he may be spared injury, if such be the Lord's will."

"Indeed we will, in that case, pour out our constant petitions for him — the dear fellow!" said Violet with emotion. "But, Levis, do you think this will bring on war?"

"It looks likely to me," replied her husband, sadness perceptible in both his countenance and tones. "And, really, I think it is our duty to interfere for those poor, savagely treated Cubans. I think it is high time that this powerful people undertook their cause."

"And I suppose the Spaniards are already angry with the Americans for sympathizing with those poor, oppressed Cubans," said Lucilla.

"Yes," said her father, "this awful deed — the blowing up of our grand battleship with its hundreds of sailors — is doubtless an expression of their ill-will."

And that was not the thought of Captain Raymond alone, but of many others as well. The wrongs and sufferings of the Cubans had so touched the hearts of thousands of Americans that they felt strongly impelled to make some effort to help them win their freedom. Now, this wanton destruction of one of our favorite battle-ships—and, what was far worse, the lives of nearly three hundred innocent men—so increased their anger and distrust that it could scarcely be restrained. Through all the land of the Americans there was a strong feeling of indignation over the treachery and cruelty of the blow that had destroyed that gallant ship and sacrificed so many innocent lives. But the people were sternly quiet while the Court of Inquiry was making its investigations. They were ready to punish the doers of that dastard-ly deed but not without proof of their guilt. For forty days they and their Congress silently awaited the report of the board of naval officers engaged in examining into the evidences of the cause of the destruction of the *Maine*. Their ver-dict came at length, but in rather vague form that, according to the evidence obtainable, the vessel had been destroyed by an explosion against her side from without. So much was clearly proven, but they did not say by whom the evil deed was done. More than a week before that report came in, both Congress and the people had been greatly moved by the speech of Senator Proctor, describing what he had witnessed in Cuba. He told of the scenes of starvation and horror and of men, women, and children robbed of their homes and cattle—all their earthly possessions — driven into the towns and left to starve to death in the streets.

The senator's fine speech made a great impression, and there were others on the same subject and in a like strain, delivered by the members of the commission sent to Cuba by the New York Journal.

Some days later — on the twenty-eighth — came the report of the Court of Inquiry into the *Maine* catastrophe and put an end to the patience of Congress, which had long been ready to undertake the cause of the long-oppressed and long- suffering Cubans.

It was not until noon of the eleventh of April that the President's message reached Congress. In that, he turned over to it the whole policy of government toward Spain. Congress did not make a formal declaration of war with Spain until the twenty-fifth of April, but the actual hostilities began on the nineteenth. Indeed, four days before the declaration of war, the United States Navy began the blockade of Cuba and captured a vessel on the high seas.

CHAPTER SEVENTH

MAX RAYMOND, buried in deep thought, was pacing the deck of the *Olympia*.

"Hello, Raymond, have you heard the news?" asked a fellow officer, hurrying toward him in evident excitement.

"No. What is it? News from home?" asked Max, pausing in his walk with a look of eager interest.

"Just that. The commodore has had a warning to leave Hong Kong. War has been declared by our government, and Great Britain has issued a proclamation of neutrality. The official warning comes from the authorities here."

"Ah!" exclaimed Max. "I knew — we all knew — that it would come soon. It is well the commodore has had all our vessels put in war paint, and every preparation made for departure upon short notice."

"Yes. Commodore Dewey is a wise man and officer. I'm glad he's at the head of affairs in this fleet. It looks as if we will have some fighting soon, Raymond."

"Yes, Dale, and it behooves us to be prepared for wounds or death. We are about to fight in a good cause, I think — for the freedom of the poor, oppressed, downtrodden Cubans. But where are we to go now? Do you know?"

They were not kept long in suspense. Presently, anchors were taken up, and with bands playing and flags flying, the fleet of vessels steamed out of the harbor, while the British residents of the city crowded the quay and shipping, cheering and saluting the Americans as the warships passed. That first voyage of the squadron was but a short one, a few miles up the coast to Mirs Bay, a Chinese harbor. There, they anchored and awaited orders from home, the *McCulloch* having been left behind to bring them when they should arrive. The next day she came, bringing this message dated Washington, April 24: "Dewey, Asiatic Squadron: War has commenced between the United States and Spain. Proceed at once to Philippine Islands. Commence operations at once, particularly against the Spanish fleet. You must capture the vessels or destroy. Use utmost endeavors.   — LONG"

This message was what Commodore Dewey had been waiting for since his arrival at Hong Kong in January. He had formed his plans and was ready to carry them out without delay. His captains were called to a short conference, and about midnight the fleet sailed on its errand of battle. They turned south toward the Philippine Islands, 620 miles away. The nearest United States port was San Francisco, 7,000 miles distant. No neutral power would permit him to take more than enough coal to carry his vessels home by the most direct route, so that there was but one course open to Dewey and his fleet — the capturing of a Spanish harbor somewhere in Asiatic waters, which he could make a naval base. One of Dewey's ships — the *Petrel* — was slow, and as the fleet of vessels must keep together, that delayed them. It was three days before they reached the line of coast of the Island of Luzon. It was reported that the enemy might be found in Subig Bay, so that was carefully reconnoitred, but the Spanish were not there. The fishermen about the harbor said they had seen no Spanish fleet, and though every nook and corner of the bay was examined, not so much as a gunboat could be found. So the American fleet passed on to Manila, thirty miles away.

It seemed evident that the Spaniards had chosen that station because there they would have the aid of short batteries. It is said that their ships were comparatively antiquated, but not so much so as to make their defeat at all certain. Their guns were as good as those of the American ships, and they had more of them. To Dewey's six fighting ships, Admiral Montojo had ten and two torpedo boats besides. The Spaniards had no vessel to rank with the *Olympia*, but the numbers of their vessels, it might have been expected, would probably, in skilled hands, have more than made up for that. The Americans had the advantage in batteries but not overwhelmingly. The *McCulloch* did not go into action at all, and the Spanish torpedo boats were sunk before their guns would bear. The Americans were greatly superior in everything that goes to win victory, but that they did not know until the fight had been going on for some time. As Commodore Dewey led his fleet along the coast of Luzon toward the harbor where he knew the enemy lay in wait for them, he had nothing less than a desperate battle to expect. The Americans were brave. We know of no cowardice among them, but to the thoughtful ones—Max Raymond among them—it was a solemn reflection that they might be nearing mutilation or sudden, painful death. The Spanish ships were anchored in a harbor protected by shore batteries. To reach them, the Americans must pass down a channel sixteen miles long guarded on each side by powerful forts armed with modern guns. It was to be expected that it held many mines prepared to blow up our vessels.

Knowing all these things, Commodore Dewey, his officers, and men must have been expecting a hard fight with no certainty of victory. There was probably but little sleep on board the vessel that night. About ten o'clock Saturday night the men were sent to their stations for battle.

Max had spent some leisure time in writing to the dear ones in his home and the still dearer one pledged to become his wife, telling just where he was and the prospect immediately before him and expressing his hope that all would go well with the Americans—now championing the cause of the poor, oppressed Cubans and of these downtrodden Filipinos. He went on to say that he would be able to write further after the conflict ended should he pass safely through it, but if he should be killed or seriously wounded, doubtless the news would reach them in due season. He told them they must think of him as having fallen in a good cause, hoping to meet them all in a better land.

A little before that, the commodore was slowly walking back and forth on the starboard side of the upper deck when he noticed an old sailor who seemed to be trying to find something to do on the port side. He was a man who had been forty years in the service of the navy and army of the United States and was a privileged character on the *Olympia*. He seemed to be keeping careful lookout on the commodore, who noticed it and perceived that he had something on his mind.

"Well, Purdy, what is it?" he asked.

Purdy straightened up and saluted. "I hope, sir," he said, "ye don't intend to fight on the third of May."

"And why not?" asked the commodore.

"Well, ye see, sir," Purdy replied in the most serious manner, "the last time I fought on the third of May I got licked — at the battle of Chancellorsville under Fighting Joe Hooker."

"All right, we won't fight on the third of May this time," said the commodore. "But when we do fight, you'll have a different kind of May anniversary to think of. Remember that, Purdy."

"Ay, ay, sir," replied Purdy, saluting and then hurrying away to rejoin his blue-jacket comrades, whom he told, "We'll lick those Spaniards if they was ten times as many as they are."

The moon was in its first quarter, and though often veiled by clouds, its light might enable the Spaniards on the fortified points here and there to perceive the stealthy approach of their foe. Max, on the watch with others, overheard the commodore say, as they neared the opening between Mariveles and the Island of Corregidor, "We ought to hear from this battery about now."

But its guns were silent. They went two miles further without perceiving any evidence that the Spaniards were even aware of their approach.

"They seem far from alert and watchful," Max presently remarked. But at that moment a bright light was thrown on the Point, an answering one was seen on the island, as if they were signaling each other. Then a rocket soared up from the center of Corregidor, and the commodore said, "It has taken them a long time to wake up, but probably they will make it all the hotter for us when they begin."

Day had not yet dawned when they reached the mouth of Manila Bay. They did not stop to reconnoiter but pressed on at once, running the gauntlet of batteries and concealed mines without waiting for daylight to make it easier.

They waited a little for the setting of the moon, then went in single file, the *Olympia* leading and the *McCulloch* bringing up the rear and with no lights except one lantern at the stern of each ship for the next to steer by.

A great light marked the entrance to the harbor, gleaming in the darkness as though to welcome the gray ships stealing so quietly in, as if to come suddenly and unexpectedly upon their prey. The forts were as silent as though all their defenders were asleep or dead. That was a wonder to the Americans, for the rush of their vessels through the water seemed to make a sound that might be heard by the enemy, and every moment they expected it to attract their attention. So anxious were they to pass unnoticed, that they spoke to each other in whispers and moved about with muffled tread. They were in momentary expectation of a cannon shot or the explosion of a mine that might rend the plates of some one of their ships, but nothing of either kind occurred until the last ship in the procession — the *McCulloch* — gave the first alarm. Coal was flung on her furnace, and a red flame flared up, lighting up the waters and the rigging of the ship itself and of those ahead. All the men on the fleet turned expectantly toward the batteries on the land, thinking that shots would certainly come now. But all was silence there. Again and again the unlucky beacon flared, and after the third time, it was noticed by the flash of a gun on a rock called El Fraile. But the aim was not good, and the shot did not strike any of our vessels. The *Concord* fired in return, and cannon roared from the *Boston*, the *McCulloch*, and again from the

Concord, but the *Olympia* and other big ships passed on in silent dignity.

The commodore was standing on the bridge of the *Olympia*, piloting his fleet, and the shot from El Fraile had given him a clear idea of how the shore lay. And now, having passed that battery, all the defenses of the harbor's mouth were left behind. Excepting mines that might lie concealed under the water, there was no further danger to meet until they should reach the city with its forts at Cavite.

As the ship steamed on up the bay, Max and Dale stood together on deck and fell into conversation.

"What ails these Spaniards?" queried Dale. "I, for one, expected nothing less than a severe fight at the very mouth of this bay, but they have let us come in and on up toward their city almost unnoticed. The strait where we came in is only about five miles wide broken by three islands, all fortified, and armed with Krupp guns. On the mainland there are two forts—one on each side—which are armed with steel-rifled cannon."

"Yes," said Max, "and we passed them all within easy range and received only ineffective fire from one battery. But this is only the beginning. At any minute we may come in contact with a mine in the channel that will explode, or an electric mine may be discharged in a way to work us serious mischief."

"True enough," said Dale. "It behooves us to be ready for the worst. There will probably be men killed and wounded on both sides."

"Yes," sighed Max. "War is an awful thing, but in this instance right is on our side, because we have undertaken the cause of the oppressed. And," he added with an effort, "if we have made our peace with God—are believing in the Lord Jesus Christ and trusting in His perfect righteousness—death will be no calamity to us. If we are wounded, no matter how painfully, He will give us strength to bear it."

"I do not doubt it," said Dale, "nor that you are in that state of preparation, Raymond. I hope I am also, and that being the case, we surely can go bravely on to meet whatever awaits us."

"I hope so," said Max, "and believing, as I do, that we are in the right, I have a strong hope that God will give us victory."

"Ah, see!" cried a voice near them. "Yonder are the Spanish ships, lying at anchor under the batteries at Cavite."

"Yes," said another. "There is the old town of Manila with its low clustering of roofs and towering cathedral."

Men crowded to the best points from which to obtain a good view and stood in silence gazing upon it. Max had a glass, and looking through it, he could see the roofs and quays of the city crowded with spectators. Evidently the engagement with the battery at El Fraile had been heard and had alarmed the city.

Dewey had made plans for a prompt fight, but he did not intend to have his men go into it hungry. Now some of his sailors were passing up and down distributing cups of hot, black coffee and biscuits.

That duly attended to, signals fluttered from the gaff. Black balls were run up to every peak on all the vessels, and, breaking out, they displayed the great battle flags. At that, some nine-inch guns on Fort Lunette were fired without doing any damage, and the American vessels suddenly moved on to closer quarters.

"Hold your fire!" was the order from the flagship, and two shots from the *Concord* was the only answer given to the forts. Onward the fleet sped toward that of the Spaniards, which was silent also. Suddenly there was a muffled roar, and a great volume of mud and water was thrown into the air right before the flagship, showing that the dreaded mines were near. In an instant, there was another explosion, but neither did any harm. Those two were all our men saw of the Spanish explosives of that sort.

Now the fleet was nearing the enemy. On the *Olympia's* bridge stood Commodore Dewey with Captain Gridley and Flag-captain Lamberton at his side. The Spanish ships now joined the forts in pouring their fire on the advancing foe, but still there was no response. Presently the sun rose red and glaring with midsummer heat, and at that the commodore, turning to the officer at his side, said quietly, "You may fire now, Gridley, when ready."

Gridley was ready, and the next instant an eight-inch shell was on its way toward the enemy, who was only about 4,500 yards distant.

Presently a signal from the flagship gave the same permission to the other vessels, and the whole fleet was engaged.

Shortly before that, Dewey had assembled the men of the *Olympia* and given them this final direction for their conduct during the fight: "Keep perfectly cool and pay attention to nothing but orders." Such was the watchword through his whole fleet that morning, and the result was a deliberate and deadly fire. The ships steamed along in regular order — the *Olympia*, the *Baltimore*, the *Raleigh*, *Petrel*, *Concord*, and *Boston* — parallel to the Spanish ships, working every gun that could be brought to bear and receiving the fire of ships and forts in return. The fire of the Spanish guns was a succession of brilliant misses — shots that came very near hitting but did not quite do so. It was, as Dewey put it in his report, "vigorous, but generally ineffective."

But the aim was not always bad. One shell struck the gratings of the bridge of the *Olympia*. One narrowly missed the commodore himself, and so hot did the fire become that he bade Captain Gridley go into the coming tower lest both of them might be killed or disabled at once. On the *Boston*, a six-inch gun was disabled, and a box of ammunition exploded. Also a shell burst in a stateroom, and set it on fire. Our six vessels steamed along down past the Spanish line, and the port side of every ship was a mass of flame and smoke. Then circling around in a grand sweep that made the Spaniards think for a moment they were pulling out of action, the column returned again on its course, and the men of the starboard batteries had a chance to try their skill while their fellows rested. They had made this circuit three times when three of the Spanish ships were on fire. Looking through glasses, the shots could be seen striking the Spanish hulls, which were thinly plated.

Admiral Montojo, stung into fury by his losses, slipped the cables of his flagship just as the Americans were beginning their third round, and under full steam he darted out as if intending to attack the *Olympia*. But as his vessel—the *Reina Christina*—swung away from her fellows, the fire of the whole American fleet was concentrated upon her. The storm of shot and shell came pouring down upon her, pierced her hull like paper, swept her decks, and spread death and destruction on every side. Her engines were pierced, and her bridge shot away. She could hardly be controlled by her helm, and as she turned her stern to the American fire, an eight-inch gun on the *Olympia* sent a projectile that struck her there and tore its way forward, exploding ammunition, shattering guns, killing men, piercing partitions, tearing up decks, and finally exploding in her after-boiler.

Agonized screams of wounded men were heard rising above the thunder of the battle, and the *Reina Christina* staggered back with flames leaping from her hatches.

While this was going on, the two Spanish torpedo boats slipped out and ran for the American fleet. One hastened toward the supply ships, but she was caught by the *Petrel*, driven ashore, and fired upon until she blew up. The other, running for the *Olympia*, was struck by a shell, broke in two, and sank out of sight.

Five times the circuit was made by the American ships. Then a signal fluttered from the yard of the *Olympia*, and the fleet turned away to the other side of the harbor, where the *McCulloch* and the colliers had been lying.

At that time the Spaniards, supposing the Americans were retreating, raised a resounding cheer. The men on the American ships were not so well pleased. They were asking what this move was for, and when told it was in order to give them their breakfast, there was more than a bit of grumbling.

"Breakfast!" exclaimed one of the gunners. "Who wants any breakfast? Why can't we finish off the Dons, now we've got them going?"

But breakfast was not what the delay was for. A misunderstood signal had made the commodore fear that the supply of ammunition for the five-inch guns on board some of the vessels was running low, and he wished to replenish their stock. It was found, however, not to be necessary. But officers and sailors had their breakfast and a three hours' rest, during which guns and machinery that had been used in that morning's fight were examined, and a supply of fresh ammunition was prepared. The signals for a renewal of the battle were given, and the ships again bore down upon the enemy, revolving as before in a great circle of smoke and fire but at a closer range than at first.

The Spaniards seemed desperate, firing wildly and in a half-hearted way. The *Reina Christina* was blown up by the shells of the *Baltimore* quickly after the *Don Juan de Austria* was destroyed by the *Raleigh*, and so on till all of the ten Spaniard ships had been destroyed or had surrendered.

Admiral Montojo had transferred his flag to the *Isla de Cuba* and fought till her guns were silenced and she was in flames. Then leaving her to her fate, he escaped to the city. It is said that a great crowd of people had come out from the city that morning to see "the pigs of Yankees" annihilated.

The last ship left fighting was the *Don Antonio de Ulloa*, and at length she sank with her flag still nailed to her mast. One of the American shots entered the magazine at Cavite, and that ended the resistance of the shore batteries. Then from the *Olympia* was flung out the signal, "The enemy has surrendered." The hot, weary, smoke-begrimed men swarmed, cheering out of the turrets and up from the bowels of the ships, and the flagship's band broke out with the *Star-Spangled Banner*, for the victory of Manila was won—the first victory of the war with Spain for the help of the sorely oppressed Cubans.

CHAPTER EIGHTH

MAX HAD DONE bravely and well, and no one rejoiced more keenly in the victory than he, though his heart bled for the wounded and slain. He as well as the others listened eagerly for the accounts of the captains of the other vessels of the fleet as they came on board to report to the commodore.

"How many killed?" was demanded of each one, as he stepped on the deck, and great was the surprise and satisfaction on learning that none had been killed.

"Only eight wounded, none seriously," was the reply of Captain Dyer of the *Baltimore*. "But six shells struck us, and two burst inboard without hurting anyone."

"Not a dashed one," was the next captain's answer. "None killed and none wounded." Said the third, "but I don't know yet how it happened. I suppose you fellows were all cut up."

"My ship wasn't hit at all," was the next report.

It was known that the *Boston* had been on fire, therefore it was expected that her captain would have to report a serious list of casualties. When he announced that no one had been killed or wounded on his vessel, the news spread quickly through the flagship, and the men cheered vociferously. The *Baltimore* had been struck by a sixty-pound projectile fired from a land battery. It struck the ship about two feet above the upper deck, between two guns that were being served; pierced two plates of steel each one-quarter of an inch thick; then ploughed through the wooden deck, striking and breaking a heavy beam, by which it was turned upward. Then it passed through a steel hatch-combing; disabled a six-inch gun; hurtled around the semicircular shield which surrounded the gun, missing the men at it; reversed its course; and traveled back to a point almost opposite that at which it had entered the ship. Thus, it passed out. It had passed between men crowded at their quarters and touched none, but it exploded some loose ammunition, by which eight were wounded.

Max listened to the accounts of the almost bloodless victory with a heart swelling with gratitude to God and full of hope for the success of America's effort to free the victims of Spanish cruelty and oppression. What glad tidings his next letter would carry to the dear ones at home. They would rejoice over the victory and his safety, too, though that might be again imperiled at any time.

This naval battle had been fought on Sunday. On Monday morning, Captain Lamberton went on shore to receive the formal surrender of the fort at Cavite. They had hauled down their flag the day before, but they now tried to prove that they had never done so. Perceiving that, the captain drew out his watch. Before leaving his ship, he had directed that unless he returned in an hour those works should be bombarded. Forty-five minutes of that hour were now gone, and he said to the Spaniards: "Unless you surrender unconditionally so soon that I can get back to my ship in fifteen minutes, the *Petrel* will open fire on your works."

That had the desired effect. They surrendered at once, and priests and nuns came humbly to beg him to refrain his men from murdering all the wounded in the hospitals. They had been told that that was the invariable practice of the barbarous "Yanquis."

The next day, the *Raleigh* and *Baltimore* went down to the mouth of the bay and, after a brief attack, captured the forts on Corregidor and Sangley Point. The guns in these works were destroyed by wrapping them with gun cotton and exploding it with electricity. The officer in command at Corregidor went aboard the *Raleigh* to surrender himself, and while there he seemed greatly alarmed to find the ship drifting in the main channel, or Boca Grand. He demanded that he be at once put ashore. Asked the reason of his alarm and haste to get away, he said the channel was full of contact mines, and though the Americans might be satisfied to brave death by them, he was not. He said it was not fair to expose a prisoner to almost certain destruction

This very same channel was the one through which the American fleet had entered the harbor.

Four days after his victory, Dewey, having all the harbor defenses at his command, sent off the *McCulloch* to Hong Kong with his first dispatches to Washington. So a week had passed after the rumors from Madrid before the American people received definite information in regard to Dewey's successes in the Philippines. These are the dispatches:

Manila, May 1—Squadron arrived Manila at daybreak this morning. Immediately engaged the enemy and destroyed following Spanish vessels: *Reina Christina, Castilla, Don Antonio de Ulloa, Isla de Luzon, Isla de Cuba, General Lezo, Marques del Duoro, El Correo, Velasco, Isla de Mindanao*, a transport and water battery at Cavite. The squadron is uninjured, and only a few men slightly wounded. Only means of telegraphing is to American consul at Hong Kong. I shall communicate with him.   —Dewey

Manila, May 4—I have taken possession of the naval station at Cavite, Philippine Islands, and destroyed the fortifications. Have destroyed fortifications at bay entrance, Corregidor Island, paroling the garrison. I control the bay completely and can take the city at any time. The squadron is in excellent health and spirits. The Spanish loss not fully known but is very heavy. One hundred and fifty killed, including captain, on *Reina Christina* alone. I am assisting in protecting Spanish sick and wounded. Two hundred and fifty sick and wounded in hospital within our lines. Much excitement in Manila. Will protect foreign residents.   —Dewey

A message of congratulation from the president and people of the United States was the immediate response to Dewey's dispatches, and with it the information that the president had thus appointed the victorious commander a rear-admiral. Doubtless a rumor concerning the nature of the dispatch quickly reached all the vessels of the fleet, for the next morning watchful eyes on many of them turned to the flagship to see what flag would be run up to the mainmast. When they saw that it was the blue flag as of yore, but it had two stars instead of one, the guns of the squadron roared out a salute to the new admiral. No one there was more rejoiced than Max, who both respected and loved his gallant commander, and no one in America felt happier over the good news in Dewey's dispatches than those to whom Max was so dear. It was a blessed relief to their anxiety to learn that no one had been killed, and none more than slightly wounded.

CHAPTER NINTH

THE SAD NEWS of the destruction of the *Maine* was quite as exciting to our friends at Ion as to those of Woodburn. All saw that war between the United States and Spain could not be long delayed, and when it was declared, both Harold and Herbert Travilla volunteered their services as physicians and surgeons to the troops to be sent to Cuba or Puerto Rico. Their mother gave her consent, though her heart bled at the thought of the toils and dangers they would be called upon to endure. But she felt that they were right in their desire to help the poor Cubans to the freedoms Americans enjoy. No one had felt deeper sympathy for the despoiled and starving reconcentradoes than she. Her sons were not going as soldiers, to be sure, but as greatly needed help to those who were to do the fighting.

Captain Raymond was strongly inclined to offer his services to the government, but he was deterred by the earnest, tearful entreaties of his wife and daughters. They urged him to refrain, for their sakes, as there seemed to be no lack of men who could be better spared — at least so it seemed to them.

"Oh, father," said Gracie, "don't think of such a thing! There are plenty of other men who can go. The poor Cubans will be sure to get free without risking the loss of the dearest father that anybody ever had."

It was shortly after breakfast on a beautiful May morning, and the whole family was together on the front veranda, the captain occupying an easy chair, while looking over the morning paper. Gracie came close to his side, and she was standing there as she spoke.

"Is that your opinion of him?" he asked, smiling up into her eyes.

"Yes, sir, and always has been," she answered, accepting a silent invitation to a seat upon his knee and putting an arm around his neck. "Oh, father, I don't know how I could live without you!" she exclaimed, her eyes filling with tears at the very thought.

"Nor I," said Lucilla. "No greater calamity than the loss of our father could possibly befall us. There are plenty of other people to look after the Cubans."

"So I think," said Violet. "If our country is in peril it would be a different matter. And, my dear, as your eldest son is in the fight—such a dear fellow as he is—I am sure that ought to be considered your full share of giving and doing for the Cuban cause."

"I should think so, indeed!" chimed in Lucilla and Gracie in a breath.

"And, oh, I can't bear to think that my brother Max may get wounded!" exclaimed Elsie.

Ned added, "And if he does, I'd just like to shoot the fellow that shoots him."

"We must try not to feel revengeful, my little son," said his father.

"Well, papa, please promise not to offer to go into the fight," pleaded Gracie, and the others all added their earnest solicitations to hers, till at length they won the desired pledge. They were too dear to the captain's heart to be denied what they pleaded for so earnestly and importunately.

Gracie was feebler and more often ailing that spring than she had been for several years before, and Dr. Arthur Conley, or one of the other of his partners—Harold and Herbert Travilla—was often there to give advice and see that it was followed. It had been Harold oftener, of late, than any one else, and he had grown very fond of the sweet girl who always listened with such deference to his advice. She called him "uncle" in her sweet voice. The thought of leaving her gave him a keener pang than anything else, as he contemplated leaving his home for the labors and dangers of the seat of war. He was glad indeed when he learned that the captain would remain at home to take care of her and the rest of his family.

Gracie noticed with pleasure that, as the time of his leaving drew near, his manner toward her grew more affectionate till it seemed almost as tender as that of her father. She thought it very nice that Uncle Harold should be so fond of her. She looked up to him as one who was very wise and good and wondered that he should care particularly for her, as she was not really related to him at all. He was fond of Lucilla also, but Gracie seemed to him the lovelier of the two. He had always been fond of her, but he did not know until he was about to leave her for the dangerous field of usefulness that his affection was of the sort to make him long for her as the partner of his life. But so it was. Yet could it be? Would the captain ever consent to such a mixture of relationships? He feared not, and at all events it was quite certain that he would not be allowed to try to win his coveted prize for years to come — she being so young and far from strong and well. Then as he was about to risk his life on the battlefields, it would be cruelty to her to try to win her love before he went.

He resolved to go without revealing his secret to any one. But he had never had an important secret from his mother. All his life he had been used to talking freely with her, telling of his hopes, aims, and wishes, his doubts and perplexities. Almost before he knew it, he had told her about enough of his feelings for Gracie that her motherly, keen-sighted affection knew how the land lay.

"Gracie is very lovely and a dear child," she said low and gently. "But, as you know, she is not well or strong. Also she is so young that her father would not hear of her marrying for years to come."

"No, mother, nor would I advise it. Unless," he added with a low, embarrassed laugh, "is was to be to a physician who would promise to take special care of her health."

"You refer to one physician in particular, I perceive," returned his mother with her low, musical laugh, laying her hand in his, for they were sitting side by side on the veranda. "Well, my dear boy, I advise you to wait till you return home before you say anything to either her or her father. But have you thought what a mixture of relationships such a marriage would make? Your brother-in-law would be also your father-in-law, and Gracie would become aunt to her own half-brother and sister."

"Yes, mother, it would cause some awkward relationships. But as there is no tie of blood between us, perhaps that need not matter. I shall say nothing till I come home and not then without the captain's permission."

"That is right. Do you think Gracie suspects your feelings for her?"

"Hardly, mother. I am only her 'uncle,' you know," Harold answered with a laugh in which there was little or no mirth.

"Although I am certainly very fond of Gracie," said his mother, "I cannot help regretting that your affections have not gone out to someone else rather than to her—because of her feeble health and the connection through your sister and her father."

"Yes, they are objections," he returned with a sigh. "But mother dear, you will not consider them insuperable if I can persuade the captain not to do so?"

"Oh, no! Not if you win, or have won, her heart. I should not think of raising the least objection, my son, and surely the captain, who is a devoted father, would not, should he see that her affections are engaged to you."

"That is my one sincere hope, mamma," said Harold. "And, as I have said, I do not intend to offer myself without his knowledge and consent, though I had hard work to refrain today when Gracie and I were left alone together for a few minutes. It was then that she expressed with tears in her sweet blue eyes such anxiety at the thought of my being in danger of wounds or death in the coming struggle with Cuba. Mother dear, Herbert and I will not, of course, be in as great danger as will the fighting men of our army and navy on the front lines, but, I suppose, that there is always a remote possibility that we may not return unharmed. In that case I should not—I would not want Gracie to know of my love and my intention to—ask her to become my wife."

"I think you are right, my son," his mother said with emotion. "But, I hope and shall pray constantly that my dear boys may come back to me unharmed from Cuba."

"It will be a great help and comfort to them to know that their dear mother's prayers are following them," rejoined Harold, tenderly pressing the hand she had laid in his.

The next moment Herbert joined them, and he, too, had a farewell talk with his mother, for the brothers were to leave for Tampa the very next morning to join the troops about to sail for Cuba.

CHAPTER TENTH

BY THE LAST OF MAY there were sixteen thousand men at Tampa under the command of General Shafter, but it was not until the fourteenth of June that they set sail for Cuba. On the clear, scorchingly hot morning of June the twenty-second, they landed at Daiquiri, twelve miles east of the entrance to Santiago Bay. From all accounts, things seem to have been woefully mismanaged, so that our poor soldiers had no facilities for landing. Those who loaded the ship, it would appear, must have been great bunglers—either exceedingly ignorant in regard to such work or most reprehensibly careless. In consequence, scarcely anything could be found when wanted. Medical stores were scattered among twelve vessels. So, when fever broke out in the trenches before Santiago, it was almost impossible to get the needed remedies. Probably—though there were never enough on the field—some medicines were left on the ships and carried back to the United States. All this made the work of the physicians doubly trying. Besides, they were too few in number, as there were many more wounded than had been expected. They were brought in faster than they could be attended to. The surgeons worked all night by the light of spluttering lamps, and there were not even enough surgical instruments. But the poor, wounded men were wonderfully brave and patient. Harold and Herbert Travilla felt that they had not engaged in a cause that did not need them. After the fighting began, their labors were exhausting—all the more so because of the drain upon their sympathies.

On the morning of July the second, the American troops were found safely entrenched on the ridge of the hill above Santiago. The day before had been one of heavy losses to our army—many officers and men killed and wounded. And now, just as light began to show in the east, the Spaniards opened a heavy fire on our works. Our men made only a few replies, for ammunition was getting scarce. So anxious about it were the soldiers that they hailed an ammunition train with great joy, though they were half starved and knew that no provisions could come while the road was crowded with such trains.

The war artist, Frederic Remington, tells of the delight with which the poor hungry fellows hailed a pack-train loaded with ammunition, though they knew that no food would be brought to them that night. "The wounded going to the rear cheered the ammunition, and when it was unpacked at the front the soldiers seized it like gold. They lifted a box in the air and dropped it on one corner, which smashed it open.

"'Now we can hold San Juan Hill against them. Hey, son?' yelled a happy cavalryman to a doughboy.

"'You bet! Until we starve to death.'

"'Starve nothin'—we'll eat them gun-teams.'"

The soldiers refilled their cartridge belts and crouched all day in trenches, watching for an assault and firing just often enough to keep the enemy from advancing upon them. While doing so, they could hear the thunder of the navy's guns far away in the southwest, where it was engaging a battery. At the same time, down in the harbor of Santiago, Cervera was getting ready to make his rush out of the harbor the next day.

The Spaniards made a dash at our men about half-past nine that night and drove them back for a few minutes from several points on their line, but they soon returned and drove the Spaniards back with heavy losses.

The next day, July third, was Sunday, and on the great ships of the American squadron, floating heavily in a half-circle about the mouth of Santiago harbor, the men were swarming on deck in fresh, clean, white clothes, ready for muster. About nine o'clock, the flagship *New York* showed the signal—"Disregard flagship's movements"—and steamed away toward the east. Admiral Sampson had gone in it for a conference with General Shafter, whose troops were then resting after their dreadful fight on San Juan Hill and El Caney.

Of our ships on watch outside the harbor, the *Brooklyn* was to the southwest, the *Texas* directly south, while the three big battleships, *Indiana*, *Iowa*, and *Oregon*, made a curve inshore east of the Morro. The little picket boat *Vixen* was there also and the *Little Gloucester* farthest east and nearest inshore. The *New York*, now absent, was the one ship supposed to be able to compete with the Spaniards in speed, and her departure left a broad gap in the blockading line.

The lookouts on the fleet had reported fires burning on the hills all the night before, and Commodore Schley, who was in command in Admiral Sampson's absence, signaled to the *Texas* the query: "What is your theory about the burning of the blockhouses on the hill last night?"

He sat on the deck waiting for an answer and at the same time watching a cloud of smoke rising from the interior of the harbor behind the hills. It did not necessarily mean anything serious, for about that time in the morning a tug was apt to make a visit to the Estrella battery. Still, they watched it, and presently the quartermaster on the forward bridge said quietly to the navigating officer, "That smoke's moving, sir." That officer took a peep himself, and what he saw nearly made him drop the glass. "Afterbridge there," he called loudly through a megaphone, "tell the commodore the enemy is coming out."

His words were heard all over the ship, and commodore, officers, sailors, and powder-boys were all rushing for their stations.

The cry rang out, "Clear ship for action," and gongs and bugles that call to general quarters clanged and pealed on the quiet air. There were echoes of the same sounds from the other ships, and the signals, "The enemy is escaping," ran to the masthead of the *Brooklyn*, the *Texas*, and the *Iowa* at the same moment, for that suspicious smoke had been watched from all the ships.

It seemed that all the vessels of the blockade had caught the alarm at the same time, and the flagship's signal was quickly changed for another: "Clear ship for action!"

But it was quite unnecessary. On every ship, men were dropping the white clothes that they had donned for general muster and hurrying to their quarters without waiting for a command. Every wooden thing was tumbled overboard; water-tight compartments were hastily shut; hose was coupled up and strung along the decks ready to fight fire; battle-hatches were lowered; and in less time than it takes to tell of it all, this was accomplished. Then at a sudden blast of a bugle, the five hundred and more men to a ship stood at their posts, each one where he would be most needed in battle and all perfectly silent. Doubtless every eye was turned toward Estrella Point where the Spanish vessels, if indeed coming out, must first show themselves. There presently a huge, black hull appeared. It came out far enough to show a turret, and from that came a flash and then the boom of a heavy shot, instantly answered by a six-pounder from the *Iowa*. The battle had begun, and "Fighting Bob" Evans had fired the first shot.

That ship just coming out was the *Maria Teresa*, and she was followed by the *Vizcaya*, the *Cristobal Colon*, and the *Almirante Oquendo*. All the American ships were standing in toward the harbor to meet them, firing rapidly from every gun that could be brought to bear. It was uncertain at first which way the Spaniards would turn when they had passed the shoals that extend half a mile beyond the mouth of the harbor. If they turned eastward they would have to run into the midst of the most formidable ships of our squadron. If they went directly west they might outrun the battleships and escape. The *Brooklyn* was the fastest ship on the blockade, and she was also in the best position to head off the Spaniards should they take that course. But it was possible she might be lost, as she was no match for the number of the enemy that would be in a position to engage her when she came up to them. Commodore Schley says that the possibility of losing his ship in that way entered very clearly into his calculations, but also that in sinking the *Brooklyn,* the Spaniards would be delayed long enough for the battleships to come up to them. Then there would be no reason to fear their escape. The difficulty was that because the *Brooklyn* was on a parallel course with the Spaniards, going in a directly opposite direction, she would have to make a complete circle in order to chase them. Had they had the speed with which they were credited, that would have put the *Brooklyn* out of the fight, one of her engines being uncoupled and in consequence her speed greatly reduced.

But the Spanish vessels fell far behind their estimated speed, so that the *Brooklyn* was able to circle about and still overhaul the fleetest of them, and the *Texas*, the very slowest of our battleships, held its own in the race.

The *Maria Teresa* passed the shoals and turned west. The little *Vixen*, lying near the *Brooklyn*, when she saw the *Maria Teresa* turn toward her, fired off her six-pounders. Then she slipped away, while the rest of the American ships came rushing down toward the enemy with their funnels belching black smoke, and turrets, hulls, and tops spurting out red flames and yellow smoke. They steamed toward the foe as fast as possible, at the same time firing fiercely from every gun that could be brought to bear and paying no attention to the shore batteries, which were firing upon them. The *Indiana* struck her more than once, but after that, the *Indiana* gave her attention to the *Vizcaya*.

By this time, all the American ships were engaged, but in the dense smoke it was almost impossible to make out how great was the success of any single one.

But Commodore Eaton, who was watching the fight from the tug *Resolute*, say: "As the *Vizcaya* came out, I distinctly saw one of the *Indiana's* heavy shells strike her abaft the funnels, and the explosion of this shell was followed by a burst of flame, which for a time obscured the after part of the stricken ship." The *Iowa* and *Oregon*, belching forth great clouds of smoke until they looked like huge yellow clouds on the water, steamed straight toward the fleeing enemy. Says Mr. Abbott: "As the battleships closed in on their prey, they overlapped each other, and careless use of the guns or failure to make out accurately the target might have resulted in one of our ships firing into another. But so skillfully were they handled, that at no time were they put in jeopardy from either guns or the rams of each other, though at one time the *Oregon* was firing right across the deck of the *Texas*."

The end of the *Maria Teresa*, the first ship to leave the harbor, came upon her very swiftly and was frightful. The shells and small projectiles searched out every part of her, spreading death and ruin and soon setting her woodwork ablaze. The scarlet flames like snakes' tongues darted viciously from her sides, but her gunners stood manfully to their guns. Little smoke hung about her, and her bold black hulk seen against the green background of the hills made her a perfect target. A shot from the *Brooklyn* cut her main water pipe, and a shell—probably from the *Oregon*—entered her hull and exploded in the engine room. A six-inch shell from the *Iowa* exploded in her forward turret, killing or wounding every man at the guns, while the storm of smaller projectiles swept her decks. The noise of their bursting made it impossible for the men to hear their officers' commands.

Admiral Cervera was on that vessel. One of his officers, telling of it afterward, said: "He expected to lose most of his ships, but he thought the *Cristobal Colon* might escape. That is why he transferred his flag to the *Maria Teresa*, so that he might perish with the less fortunate." And this is the story told to an American journalist by another officer who stood by the admiral's side while that dreadful fight was on. Of a shell from the *Brooklyn*, he said: "It struck us in the bow, ploughing down amidships. Then it exploded. It tore down the bulkheads, destroyed stanchions, crippled two rapid-fire guns, and killed fifteen or twenty men." Of a shell from the *Iowa* he said: "It struck the eleven-inch gun in the forward turret of the cruiser, cutting a furrow as clean as a knife out of the gun. The shell exploded halfway in the turret, making the whole vessel stagger and shake in every plate. When the fumes and smoke had cleared away so that it was possible to enter the turret, the other gunners were sent there. The survivors tumbled the bodies that filled the wrecked turret through the ammunition hoist to the lower deck. Even the machinery was clogged with corpses. All our rapid-fire guns aloft soon became silent, because every gunner had been either killed or crippled at his post and lay on the deck where he fell. There were so many wounded that the surgeons ceased trying to dress wounds. Shells had exploded inside the ship, and even the hospital was turned into a furnace. The first wounded who were sent there had to be abandoned by the surgeons, who fled for their lives from the intolerable heat."

The *Teresa* came under the fire of our guns about 9:35 that morning. Fifteen minutes later, smoke was rising from her ports and hatches, showing that she had been set afire by the American shells. The shot from the *Brooklyn* that cut her water main made it impossible to extinguish the flames, and the fire from the American ships grew more accurate and deadly every minute. So she was beached, and her flag hauled down in token of surrender.

The men on the *Texas* raised a shout of joy. But Captain Philip spoke from the bridge: "Don't cheer, men. Those poor fellows are dying."

For less than forty minutes, Admiral Cervera had been running a race for life, and now, clad in underclothes, he tried to escape to the shore on a raft directed by his son. But he was captured and taken by the *Little Gloucester*, where he was received with the honors due his rank. His voyage from Santiago had been just six miles and a half but had cost the lives of nearly half his officers and crew.

The *Vizcaya* had followed the *Teresa* at a distance of about eight hundred yards in coming out of Santiago harbor. Upon her decks, in Havana harbor. Spanish officers had looked down with careless indifference upon the sunken wreck of our gallant battleship, the *Maine*, and it may be supposed that when she came ploughing out of the bay, Wainwright, late of the *Maine*, now on the *Little Gloucester*, aimed some shots at her with a special ill-will. But the *Vizcaya*, under gathered headway, rushed on to the west, passing the heavier battleships *Iowa* and *Indiana* and receiving terrible punishment from their guns. A lieutenant of the *Vizcaya*, taken prisoner to the United States, in an interview by a newspaper reporter, told of the murderous effect of the shells from the *Indiana*.

"They appeared to slide along the surface of the water and hunt for a seam in our armor," he said. "Three of those monster projectiles penetrated the hull of the *Vizcaya* and exploded there before we started for the shore. The carnage inside the ship was something horrible and beyond description. Fires were started constantly. It seemed to me that the iron bulkheads were ablaze. Our organization was perfect. We acted promptly and mastered all small outbreaks of flame until the ammunition magazine was exploded by a shell. From that moment, the vessel became a furnace of fire. While we were walking the deck headed shoreward, we could hear the roar of the flames under our feet above the voice of the artillery. The *Vizcaya's* hull bellowed like a blast furnace. Why, men sprang from the red-hot decks straight into the mouths of sharks."

But the *Vizcaya* lasted longer than the *Almirante Oquendo*, which followed her out of the harbor. The *Vizcaya* turned at the mouth of the harbor and went west, the *Brooklyn*, *Oregon*, and *Texas* in hot pursuit, while the *Indiana* and *Iowa* attacked the *Oquendo*. She had been credited with as great speed as that of her sister ships, but this day moved so slowly that she fared worse than any other of her comrades. She stood the fire of her foes five minutes longer than that of the *Teresa*. Then, with flames poring out of every opening in her hull, she ran for the beach, hauling down her flag as she went in token of surrender, while at the same time men were dropping from her red hot decks into the water.

Thus, in the first three-quarters of an hour, two great Spanish war vessels were destroyed, and the American fleet was concentrating its fire on the remaining two.

The fighting men on the vessels were not the only ones who did noble work for their country that day. In the engine rooms and stoke holes of the men-of-war, on that scorching hot July day, men worked naked in fiery heat. They could hear the thunder of the guns above them and feel the ship tremble with the shock of the broadsides. How the battle was going, they could not see. Deep in their fiery prison, far below the lapping waves that rushed along the armored hull, they only knew that if disaster came they would suffer first and most cruelly. Even a successful torpedo stroke would mean death to them—in fact, every one. The clean blow of an enemy's ram would in all probability drown them like rats in a cage, even if it did not cause them to be parboiled by the explosion of their own boilers. A shot in the magazine would be their death warrant. All the perils that menaced the men who were fighting so bravely at the guns on deck threatened the sooty, sweating fellows who shoveled coal and fixed fires down in the hold with the added certainty that for them escape was impossible and the inspiration that comes from the very sight of the battle was denied them. They did their duty nobly. If we had not the testimony of their commanders to that effect, we still should know it, for they drew out of every ship not only the fullest speed with which she was credited under the most favorable circumstances, but even more. This was most notable in the cases of the *Texas* and *Oregon*, which, despite bottoms fouled from long service in tropical waters, actually exceeded their highest recorded speed in the chase. On the *Oregon*, when she was silently pursuing the *Colon* at the end of the battle, Lieutenant Milligan, who had gone down into the furnace room to work by the side of the men on whom so much depended, came up to the captain to ask that a gun might be fired now and then. "My men were almost exhausted," said Milligan, "when the last thirteen-inch gun was fired. The sound of it restored their energy, and they fell to work with renewed vigor. If you will fire a gun occasionally it will keep their enthusiasm up." On most of the ships, the great value of the work the men in engine rooms were doing was recognized by the captain's sending down every few minutes to them an account of how the fight progressed. Each report was received with cheers and redoubled activity.

On the *Brooklyn*, when the *Colon* was making her final race for life, Commodore Schley sent orderlies down to the stoke holes and engine room with this message: "Now, boys, it all depends on you. Everything is sunk except the *Colon*, and she is trying to get away. We don't want her to, and everything depends on you." The *Colon* did not get away.

The *Vizcaya* was still making a gallant running fight, and in some degree protecting the magnificent *Cristobal Colon*. While these fled, disaster fell upon the two torpedo boat destroyers, *Pluton* and *Furor*. Instead of dashing at the nearest American ship—which would have been their wisest course—both followed the example of the cruisers and turned along the shore to the westward. Either of them would have been more than a match for the *Little Gloucester*, but her commander, Richard Wainwright, sped forward in a cloud of smoke from her own guns, receiving unnoticed shots from the batteries and the nearer Spanish cruisers, though one six-inch shell would have destroyed her. The batteries of the

Pluton and *Furor* were of twice the power of the *Little Gloucester's*, and they had, besides, the engine of destruction that they could send out from their torpedo tubes. But in a few minutes, Wainwright was engaged with them both at short range and under fire of the Socapa battery. The other American battleships had been firing at them, but they desisted when they perceived that the *Little Gloucester* alone was capable of managing them. In a very few minutes, they both began to smoke ominously, and their fire became much less rapid. Then the *Furor* moved as if her steering gear had been cut. Wainwright and his men redoubled their efforts at the guns. Suddenly, on the *Furor*, amidships, there shot up a great cloud of smoke and flame with a deafening roar and a shock that could be felt across the water, even amid the thunders of the guns. A shell from one of the battleships had struck her fairly and broken her in two, exploding either the magazine or the boilers, or both, and she sank like a stone.

Wainwright then pursued the other torpedo boat, the *Pluton*, more vigorously. She was already badly crippled and tried hard to escape. But at last, fairly shot to pieces, she hauled down her flag and ran for the line of breaking surf, where her men leaped overboard to escape the fierce flames that were sweeping relentlessly below from bow to stern.

The sight of their danger and distress changed Wainwright from a pitiless foe to a helping friend. He manned his boats and went to the rescue of those still alive on the burning ship. Many were saved, and the Americans had hardly left the smoking ship when it blew up with a resounding roar and vanished as had its companion. Just forty minutes they had lasted under the American fire and without being at any time a serious menace to our ships.

The entire battle had now lasted for about three-quarters of an hour. The *Infanta Maria Teresa* and the *Oquendo* were blazing on the beach with their colors struck. The battleship *Indiana* had been signaled to turn in toward the shore and give aid to the survivors on the burning ships. Only two Spanish vessels were left— the *Vizcaya*, running and fighting bravely in a hopeless struggle for life, and the *Cristobal Colon*, which was rushing at great speed down the coast to the westward. In the chase of these two vessels, the *Brooklyn* held the place of honor. Her position on the blockade at the time that the enemy came out was a commanding one, and her speed kept her well to the front. At the beginning of the fight, the *Texas* was next to her. In this battle, she developed marvelous speed and fought with reckless gallantry. The *Oregon* was third at the start, but by a wonderful dash, she passed the *Texas* and actually caught up with the *Brooklyn*, whose tars turned out on deck to cheer her—the wonderful fighter from the Pacific coast dockyard. The *Iowa* was only a short distance in their rear, and the fire of the four now concentrated upon the unhappy *Vizcaya*, which had escaped serious injury while the attention of the entire American fleet was given to the *Oquendo* and the *Teresa*, but now with four of the best fighting machines in the world devoting their entire attention to her, she began to go to pieces. The heavy shells and smaller projectiles that struck her made a great clangor and caused her great frame to quiver. When an hour had passed, the *Brooklyn*, *Oregon*, and *Texas* were the only ones pursuing her. The *Indiana* had been left behind, and the *Iowa* had stopped to aid the burning and drowning men on the blazing warships. The fire of the three warships was concentrated on the *Vizcaya* only. They were scarcely more than half a mile from her, and the effect of the shots began to tell. One of the *Brooklyn* gunners reported to the lieutenant who had charge of that turret that he didn't see any of the shots dropping into the water. "Well, that's all right," replied the officer. "If they don't drop into the water, they are hitting." And so they were. The beautiful woodwork inside of the vessel was all in a blaze. The hull was pierced below the water line; the turrets were full of dead and wounded men; and the machinery was shattered. Captain Eulate, her commander, was a brave officer and a gentleman, but he found himself compelled to abandon the fight, so turned his ship's prow toward that rocky shore on which lay the wrecks of the *Oquendo*, the *Teresa*, and the *Furor*.

As the *Vizcaya* swung about, a shell from the *Oregon* struck her fairly in the stern. An enormous mass of steel, charged with explosives of frightful power, it rushed through the steel framework of the ship, shattering everything in its course, crashed into the boiler, and exploded. Words are powerless to describe the ruin that resulted. Men, guns, projectiles, ragged bits of steel and iron, splinters, and indescribable debris were hurled in every direction, while flames shot up from every part of the ship. A fierce fire raged between her decks, and those who were gazing at her from the decks of the American men-of-war could see what looked like a white line reaching from her bow to the water, which was in fact the men dropping one after another over the side to seek the cool relief of the ocean from the fiery torment they were enduring.

The *Colon* was now left alone and was doing her utmost to escape. The men on our foremost pursuing ships soon perceived that there could be no hope of escape for her. Commodore Schley saw it and began to lighten the strain on his men. They were called out on the superstructure to see what had been done by the guns of the fleet and to watch the chase. They came pouring out from the turrets, up from the engine rooms and magazines — stalwart fellows, who were smoke-begrimed and sweaty. Almost abeam they saw the *Vizcaya* with men dropping from every port. Far astern were the smoking wrecks of the *Teresa* and *Oquendo*, ahead on the right was the *Colon*, fleeing for her life, while the *Brooklyn* rushed after her relentlessly.

As the men crowded along the decks and on the turret top, they suddenly and spontaneously sent up a cheer for the Admiral. The Admiral, on the bridge above them, looked down upon them with moistened eyes. "They are the boys who did it," he said to one who stood beside him, and he spoke truly.

Then the men cheered the *Oregon*, which was coming up gallantly, and her men returned the cheer. Now all felt that even the last of Cervera's vessels was sure to be soon taken, and signals of a social and jocular character were exchanged. One from the *Brooklyn* suggested to the *Oregon* that she try one of her thirteen-inch guns on the chase. The great cannon flashed and roared from the forward turret, and the shell, which rushed passed the *Brooklyn* with a noise like a railway train, fell short. On they rushed, the *Oregon* visibly gaining on the fastest ship of the Spanish navy—a battleship built for weight and solidity overhauling a cruiser built for speed! Another shell was sent, and it fell so near the *Colon* that the captain seemed to read in it the death warrant of his ship. He turned her toward the shore and beached her, hauling down his flag as she struck. Captain Cook went in a boat to take possession of the prize, his crew being ordered not to cheer or exult over the vanquished. The *Colon* surrendered at 1:10P.M., ending a naval battle that lasted less than four hours and possessed many extraordinary and unique qualities. It completed the wreck of Spanish naval power and dealt the decisive stroke that deprived Spain of her last remnant of American colonies. It was of absorbing interest to naval experts in all parts of the world, and it was unique in that while the defeated fleet lost six ships, more than six hundred men killed and drowned, and eighteen hundred prisoners, many of them wounded, the victors had but one man killed and one wounded.

No wonder that when the fight was over, the victory won—such a victory, too—a Christian man, such as Captain Philip of the *Texas*, whose crew were cheering in a very delirium of joy, should call them about him, and, uncovering his head, say in a reverential tone: "I want to make public acknowledgment here that I believe in God, the Father. I want you all to lift your hats and from your hearts offer silent thanks to the Almighty."

And truly they had abundant reason for great thankfulness, having escaped with so few casualties, while the foe had suffered so terribly. Scores of the Spanish were being literally roasted alive, for the whole interior of the ships—*Vizcaya*, *Oquendo*, and *Teresa*—became like iron furnaces at white heat. Even the decks were red hot, and the wounded burned where they lay. So crazed by the sight of the agony of men wounded and held fast by the jamming of the gratings, were some of those otherwise unhurt, that they could hardly be induced to respond to efforts for their own rescue. They would cling to a ladder or the side of a scorching hot ship and have to be literally dragged away before they would loose their hold and drop into a boat below. Our sailors worked hard on blistering decks amid piles of ammunition that were continually being exploded by the heat and under guns that might at any minute send out a withering blast, risking life and limbs in succoring their defeated foes. It is not too much to say that in that work of mercy, the bluejackets encountered dangers quite as deadly as those they had met in the fury of battle.

The poor marksmanship of the Spaniards saved our ships from being damaged, but a good many shots struck. The *Brooklyn* bore in all some forty scars of the fight, twenty-five of them having been shells, but she was so slightly injured that she could have begun all over again when the *Colon* turned over on the shore. The *Iowa* was hit twice, the *Texas* three times, one shell smashing her chart house and another making a hole in her smokestack. The injuries to the other ships were of even less importance.

CHAPTER ELEVENTH

THE VERY MORNING that Cervera attempted his flight from Santiago, General Shafter sent into the Spanish lines by a flag of truce a demand for the surrender of the city. "I have the honor to inform you," he said, "that unless you surrender I shall be compelled to shell Santiago de Cuba. Please instruct the citizens of all foreign countries and all women and children that they should leave the city before ten in the morning tomorrow."

That flag of truce had been gone only two or three hours when there came a sudden rumor that the Spanish fleet had gone to destruction, depriving Santiago of her chief defense. Our soldiers were so sure of the prowess of our sailors, that they hailed the rumor as fact—as news of a victory. When later in the evening the actual intelligence of Schley's glorious triumph reached them, they went wild with joy and danced on the crest of the defenses in full view of the Spaniards, venturing to do so because—as there was a truce—no jealous sharpshooter would dare to fire on them. The band played patriotic and popular airs, particularly "There'll be a Hot Time in the Old Town Tonight." Bonfires were made and salutes fired.

Drs. Harold and Herbert Travilla, wearied with their labors for the sick and wounded, rejoiced as heartily as any one else over the good news, yet at the same time they felt pity for the suffering of those of the foe who had perished so miserably by shot, shell, and fire. They would have been glad to aid the wounded prisoners, but their hands were already full in giving attention to our men so sorely injured by Spanish shot and shell. So incessant and arduous had been their labors in that line and so fierce and exhausting was the heat, that they were themselves well nigh worn out. There had been hope that the city would surrender, but on the night of the third—the day of the naval battle—four thousand fresh Spanish troops entered it. So, the hoped-for surrender was not made.

The Americans in the trenches were hot, hungry, and water-soaked, and some of them grew very impatient. Said one of the Rough Riders, "Now that we've got those 'em corralled, why don't we brand them?"

On the sixth, something happened that broke the monotony and gave great joy to the soldiers in the trenches. A cavalcade of men was seen coming from the beleaguered city, the first of whom was quickly recognized as Lieutenant Hobson, who with his seven comrades had gone out one night, weeks before, on a vessel, the *Merrimac*, to sink her across the narrow entrance to the channel leading into Santiago harbor and so bottle up the Spanish fleet.

They failed, and were taken prisoners by the Spaniards, and had been spending weeks shut up in Morro castle. Now they had been exchanged for seven prisons taken at San Juan. At sight of them, the American soldiers seemed to go mad with joy. They yelled, danced, laughed, and even wept for joy. Then the band on the foremost line struck up *The Star-Spangled Banner,* and all stood silent at a salute. But the moment the music ceased, it seemed as if Bedlam had broken loose. The regulars crowded about the heroes, cheering them, shaking them by the hand, while they from their ambulance yelled compliments and congratulations to the tattered and dirty soldiers.

When those returned sailors reached the fleet after dark, they found the ships' companies turned out as if to greet an admiral at least, coming to visit them, and as their launch was seen approaching from the shore the cheers of their brother tars made the hills of Cuba ring almost as had the thundering fire of Morro and Estrella when leveled against them nearly six weeks before.

The surrender of Santiago took place on the eighteenth of July. By that time, there was a great deal of sickness among our troops, and Harold and Herbert Travilla were kept busy attending to the sick and wounded. So overworked were they and so injuriously affected by the malarious climate, that both became ill. Herbert became so ill that he could scarcely keep about, and his brother began to question whether it was not his duty to take or send him home, or even farther north, to join their mother and a number of relatives and connections who were spending the summer on the Hudson or at some Northern seaside resort. He was at liberty to do so, as the two of them were serving as volunteer surgeons and without pay.

On the morning after the surrender, Herbert found himself entirely unfit for duty, and on his account Harold felt much depressed as he went through the hospital examining and prescribing for his patients. Presently he heard a quick, manly step and a familiar voice saying in cheery tones, "Good morning, Harold! How are you?"

The young doctor turned quickly with the joyous exclamation, "Why, Brother Levis! Can it be possible that this is you?" holding out his hand in a cordial greeting as he spoke.

"It is not only possible but an undeniable fact," returned Captain Raymond with his pleasant smile, giving the offered hand a warm, brotherly pressure.

"And you came in your yacht? Have some of the family come with you — my mother —"

"Oh, no!" returned the captain quickly. "At present, it is much too warm for her — or any other of our lady friends — in this locality. She and our family are at Crag Cottage, and by her request I have come to take you and Herbert aboard the *Dolphin* and carry you to her. I didn't come alone. Your brothers Edward and Walter are with me, and your cousin Chester also."

"Oh, what delightful news!" exclaimed Harold, his eyes shining with joy. "Your yacht is here?"

"Lying down yonder in the harbor, just waiting for two additions to her list of passengers. But where is Herbert?" looking about as if in search of him.

"Lying in our tent on the sick list, the poor, dear fellow!" sighed Harold. "Can you wait five minutes for me to get through here for the present? Then I will take you to him."

"Certainly, longer than that, if necessary. Ah, I see it was time—high time—for me to come for you boys."

Harold smiled in a rather melancholy way at that comment.

"I have grown to feel quite old since we have been here in the midst of so much suffering and been obliged to take so heavy a load of care and responsibility—performing serious operations and the like," he said with a sigh. "I must find you a seat," he added, glancing about in search of one.

"No, no," the captain hastened to say. "I should prefer walking around here and making acquaintance with some of these poor, brave fellows—if you think it would not be unpleasant to them."

"I think they would be pleased to have you do so," was Harold's reply.

A few minutes later he and the captain went into the tent where Herbert lay in a burning fever. The very sight of the captain and the news that he had come to carry him and Harold north to a cooler climate, their mother, and other dear ones seemed so greatly to revive him that he insisted upon being considered quite able to be taken immediately on board the yacht, and his brother and brother-in-law promptly set about preparations to carry out his wish.

"You will go, too, Harold?" he said inquiringly to his brother.

"To the *Dolphin*? Yes, certainly, old fellow. You are my patient now, and I must see to it that you are well accommodated and cared for," returned Harold in a sprightly tone.

"And you are going with me to see to that throughout the voyage?"

"I don't know," Harold returned in a tone of hesitation. "These poor, wounded, sick fellows—"

"You'll be down on your back as sick as any of them if you stay here another week," growled Herbert. "And with nobody to take care of you, you'll die, and that'll break mother's heart. As you are working without pay, you've a right to go as soon as you will."

"Yes," said the captain, "and if you fall sick you'll be no service but only in the way. Better let me attend to the necessary arrangements for you and carry you off along with your brother."

After a little hesitation, Harold consented to that, saying that after seeing Herbert on board the yacht he would return, make all necessary arrangements, bid good-bye to his patients, then board the *Dolphin* for the homeward voyage.

"That's right, brother mine," Herbert said with a pleased smile. "I'd be very unwilling to go, leaving you here alone. What would mother say?"

It took but a few minutes to pick up their few belongings, and they were soon on the deck of the yacht receiving the warm greetings of their brothers and cousin. Their family members were greatly concerned over their weary and haggard look.

"You are worn out, lads," said Edward, "and the best and kindest thing we can do will be to carry you up north to a cooler climate and to mother and the others, who will, I hope, be able to soon nurse you back to health and strength."

"So say I," said Chester.

"And I," added Walter. "I have always found mother's nursing the best to be had anywhere or from any body."

"Yes," said the captain. "And there are sisters and others to help with it at Crag Cottage, where I hope to land you a few days hence."

In a brief time, Herbert had been comfortably established in one of the staterooms and left in Edward's charge, while Harold went ashore to make his farewell visit to his hospital patients. Chester and Walter accompanied the captain in paying a visit to some of the men-of-war officers who were old acquaintances and chums of the last-named when he belonged to the navy.

It was most interesting to them all to see both the men and the vessels that had taken part in that remarkable battle and to hear accounts of its scenes from the actors in them. In fact, so much interested were they that Captain Raymond said he could not have Edward and Harold miss it. He arranged to have them visit the vessels later, leaving Chester and Walter in charge of Herbert, since he was too ill to accompany them.

That afternoon the plan was carried out, and that night the *Dolphin* started on her return voyage to the north. The change from the rough camps on Cuban soil to the luxurious cabin of the *Dolphin* was very agreeable and refreshing to the young volunteer physicians, but they were too thoroughly worn out with their toils, anxieties, and privations for even so great and beneficial a change to work an immediate cure. They were still on the sick list when they reached Crag Cottage.

CHAPTER TWELFTH

EVELYN'S DESIRE had been to add to Crag Cottage over the past years. Now, it could accommodate a large number of guests. There were so many who were near and dear to her and whom she loved to gather about her that she could not be content till this was done. Now the families of Fairview, Ion, and Woodburn were all spending the summer there along with Ronald Lilburn and Annis, his wife. Several of the gentlemen had gone to Cuba to learn of the welfare of Harold and Herbert Travilla about whom their mother had grown very solicitous. They had been gone long enough for hopes to be entertained of their speedy return, but there was no certainty in regard to the time of their arrival at the cottage.

It was late in the afternoon. The elder people were gathered on the front porch overlooking the river, most of the younger ones amusing themselves about the grounds. Grandma Elsie was gazing out upon the river with a slightly anxious expression of countenance.

"Looking for the *Dolphin*, mamma?" asked her daughter Violet.

"Yes. Though it is hardly time to expect her yet, I fear."

"Oh, yes, mamma, for there she is now!" exclaimed Violet, springing to her feet in her delight and pointing to a vessel passing up the river, which had just come into sight.

Many of those on the porch and the young folks on the grounds had also caught sight of her, and a joyous shout was raised, "The *Dolphin*! The *Dolphin*! There she is! The folks have come!"

"Oh, can we run down and get aboard her, mamma?" asked Elsie Raymond. "I'm in such a hurry to see papa and get a kiss from him."

"You won't have long to wait for that, I am sure," returned her mother with a smile. "But it will be better to wait a few minutes and get it here. There are so many of us that if we should all go down to the landing we would be very much in the way."

Others thought the same, and the ladies and children waited where they were while Mr. Leland and Edward, his oldest son, went down the winding path that led to the little landing place at the foot of the hill to greet friends on board the yacht and give any assistance that might be needed.

They found all well but the two doctors, Harold being able to walk up to the house with the help of a sustaining arm but Herbert having to be borne on a litter. The mother's heart ached at sight of his wan cheeks and sunken eyes, but he told her the joy of her presence and loving care would soon work a change for the better. He was speedily carried to a comfortable bed, and everything done to cheer, strengthen, and relieve him.

Nor was Harold's reception any less tenderly affectionate and sympathizing. His mother was very glad that he was not so ill as his brother and hoped the pure air and cooler climate would soon restore him to his wonted health and strength.

"I hope so, mother dear," he said, forcing a playful tone and smile, "and that they will soon do as much for Herbert also. He, poor fellow, is not fit to be up at all, and I think it will be well for me to retire early."

"You must do just what you deem best for your health, my dear boy," said his mother. "But shall I not send for a physician, as I fear neither of you is well enough to manage the case of the other?"

"No, no, mother, please don't!" exclaimed Herbert. "Harold is well enough to prescribe for me, and I prefer him to any other doctor."

"As I should, if he were quite well," she said, regarding Harold with a proud, fond smile, which he returned.

"My trouble is more to do with weariness than any serious illness, mother, and I hope a few days of rest here in the pleasant society of relatives and friends will quite restore me to wonted health and vigor," Harold responded in cheerful tones.

"I hope so, indeed," she said, "and that Herbert may not be far behind you in recovering his."

In the meantime joyful greetings were being exchanged among the relatives and friends upon the porch, and the returned travelers were telling of what they had seen and heard in their absence, especially on the coast of Cuba. It was all very interesting to the auditors, but the tale was not half told when the tea bell summoned them to their evening meal.

Chester had a good deal more to tell Lucilla as they wandered about the grounds together after leaving the table. And she was greatly interested.

"I should like to get aboard a battleship," she said, "particularly the *Oregon*. What a grand vessel she must be!"

"It is," said Chester, "and did grand work in that battle. I'm sure it is a battle that will go down in history as a most remarkable one. I am proud of the brave tars who fought it and not less so of the fine fellows who kept up the fires under the engines, which were as necessary to the gaining of the victory as was the firing of the guns."

"But, oh, the terrible carnage!" exclaimed Lucilla with a shudder.

"Yes, that was awful, but what a wonder— what a cause for gratitude to God—that only one was killed and so few were badly wounded on our ships."

"Yes, indeed! And truly I believe that was because we were fighting for the deliverance of the downtrodden and oppressed. Don't you believe that, too, Chester?"

"Most assuredly I do," came his emphatic rejoinder. "Has there been any news from Manila?" he asked presently.

"No," she said, "but we are looking every day for a letter from Max. Oh, I hope he is still unharmed! That victory of Dewey's seems to me to have been as great and wonderful as this later one at Santiago."

"So I think. Ah, Lu, darling, I do so wish Max might be ordered home soon, both for his own sake and ours."

"Yes, but try to be patient," she returned in a light and cheery tone. "I am sure we are having pleasant times as things are, and we are young enough to wait, as my father says. I am still almost three years younger than he thinks a girl ought to be to undertake the cares of married life."

"I don't mean for you to have much care, and I am sure you are fully capable of all you would be called upon to do. My darling, if you don't have an easy life it shall be from no fault of mine."

"I am sure of that, Chester, and I am not in the least afraid to trust my happiness to your keeping. But I am willing to wait somewhat longer to please father and to have Max present—especially as Eva's bridegroom. Oh, I think a double wedding will be just lovely!"

"If one didn't have to wait for it," sighed Chester. "Yet it is a great consolation that we can be together pretty nearly every day in the year."

"Yes, you are a very attentive suitor, and I appreciate it."

Later in the evening, when most of the guests had retired to their apartments for the night, the captain and his daughter had a bit of private chat upon the porch, for she still retained her love for that, and it was hardly less enjoyable to him.

"You don't know how I missed our usual bit of private talk with you, father, while you were away on your little trip," she said with a loving look up into his eyes as she stood by his side with his arm about her waist.

"Probably not more than I did, daughter mine," he returned, stroking her hair caressingly, then pressing his lips to her forehead and cheek. "Pacing the deck alone, I missed my little girl more than I can tell her."

"Ah, didn't you almost wish you had granted my request to be allowed to go along with you?" she asked with a pleased little laugh.

"No, my child. You are too great a treasure for me willingly to expose you to the risks of such a voyage at such a time."

"You, dear father! You are so kindly careful of me and of all your children."

"It behooves a man to be very careful of his treasures," he said. "I should have greatly enjoyed your companionship, daughter, if I could have had it without risk to you."

"I should have liked to see the warships and the scene of the battle," she said. "What a terrible battle it was, father, for the Spaniards, at least."

"Yes," he sighed. "May the time soon come when men shall learn war no more but shall beat their swords into ploughshares and their spears into pruning hooks."

"It doesn't seem as though that time can be very near," she said. "Papa, do you think Max is in much danger there in Manila?"

"I hardly know, daughter. I hope we shall hear from him soon. I hardly think there will be much, if any more, fighting for him to do there at present. But his next letter will probably enable us to judge better about that."

"Oh, I hope it will come soon!" she exclaimed in a tone of ardent desire.

"As I do," he sighed. "I cannot but feel anxious for my dear boy—though the worst seems to be over there as well."

The next morning's mail brought the desired letters to father, sisters, and ladylove. The captain's gave news of the doings of the army and navy, and after a private perusal he read the greater part of it aloud to the family and friends. It told of the irksomeness of their situation, the weariness of the watching and waiting for troops that did not come, the admiral's patience and forbearance in taking the delay so quietly, the troubles with the insurgents under Aguinaldo, and the commanders of the warships of several European nations. "'We know,'" he said, "'that those fellows are looking out for the first sign of weakness on our part or the first disaster that might befall us, intending to take advantage of it to intervene. I can tell you, father, that Admiral Dewey is a credit to his country and that country's navy. He is very kindhearted and takes excellent care of his men. He is gentle, kind to all, but thorough, determined, and energetic. Everything under his control must be as perfect as possible. When it comes to the necessity for fighting, he believes in being most thoroughly prepared and striking quick, hard blows, soon putting the enemy in a condition where they cannot fight. He says little or nothing about what he expects, but he seems to be always ready for whatever happens. The behavior of the foreign ships must be a constant worry to him, though he says little or nothing about it. The Germans here seem to study methods of annoying us. Their ships are constantly coming in or going out of Manila Bay at all hours and on the most frivolous pretexts. Sometimes they come in at night in a way that makes our lookouts think them Spanish torpedo boats. Should we send a shot at one of them, it might cause the gravest international complications. And the German naval officers make the Spanish officers their chosen companions.

"'The other day our admiral learned that one of the German vessels had violated neutrality by landing provisions in Manila. He summoned the flag lieutenant to his cabin, and when the officer came, "Oh, Brumby," he said, "I wish you to take the barge and go over to the German flagship. Give Admiral von Diederich my compliments and say that I wish to call his attention to the fact that the vessels of his squadron have shown an extraordinary disregard of the usual courtesies of naval interaction. Finally, tell him that one of them has committed a gross breach of neutrality in landing provisions in Manila, a port which I am blockading."

"'The Admiral spoke in a very quiet, gently modulated voice, but as the lieutenant turned to go, he called him back and added in a wrathful tone, "And, Brumby, tell Admiral von Diederich that if he wants a fight, he can have it right now."

"'The message had the desired effect, and we have had much less annoyance from the Germans since.

"'The English squadron here is equal to the German, and I am glad to be able to say that the British officers lose no opportunity to show their friendship for us. I am told that the German admiral asked Captain Chichester, the British commander, what the English would do in case the Germans should protest against an American bombardment of Manila. That messenger received this answer: "Say to Admiral von Diederich that he will have to call on Admiral Dewey to find out what the British ships will do in that event. Admiral Dewey is the only man authorized to answer that question." I cannot vouch for the exact truthfulness of this report,'" the captain went on reading Max's letter, "'but I can comment on the hostility of the Germans and the friendliness of the English. And we hear reliable reports of sailors' fights in Hong Kong, in which British and Yankee blue-jackets fight shoulder to shoulder against German seamen subject to the Kaiser.'"

"Oh, that is good!" exclaimed Lucilla, as her father paused in his reading. "I hope we and the British will always be friends after this. Don't you think, father, that joining together, we could rule the world?"

"Yes, and I hope, with you, that we may always be friends. Though it is not necessary that we should always take part in each other's quarrels."

"I hope Max is well?" said Violet inquiringly.

"Yes," said his father. "He tells me he is, and that he came through the battle without the slightest wound."

"I hope the President will let Dewey come home soon and Brother Max with him," said little Elsie. "Doesn't Max say anything about that, papa?"

"No, my child, except that he fears it will be months, if not years, before we see each other again. But we won't despair. It may be that the war will be short and peace will return our dear boy to us sooner than now seems likely."

The captain seemed to have finished reading the part of Max's letter that he thought best for all to hear, and he was folding it up. "Mother," he said, turning to Mrs. Travilla, "the air out here is delightful this morning. Don't you think it might do Harold good to lie yonder in the hammock?

He could come out with the assistance of my arm, I think."

"I certainly do," she said. "Thank you for your kind offer. Both he and Herbert will be deeply interested in the contents of Max's letter, if you are willing to let them see or hear it."

"Certainly, mother," the captain hastened to say. "I will carry it in and read it to them before we bring Harold out."

And he did just that. They were both greatly interested, and upon the conclusion of the reading, Harold was glad to accept the offer of the captain to help him out to the porch and into a hammock, where he could lie at ease and enjoy the companionship of other members of the party, older and younger. They were all ready to wait upon him and to do whatever they could for his comfort and entertainment. None more so than Gracie, whose ministrations he seemed to prefer to any other. As the days went on they were often left alone together, while husbands and wives and lovers devoted themselves to each other. Mrs. Travilla nursed her sicker son, and Evelyn tended to her housekeeping and correspondence, especially her letters to Max, her affianced.

Gracie was fond of Harold, as she thought any one might be of so kind an uncle, whose medical skills had many times relieved suffering for her and who had always shown kindly sympathy in her ailments. She wanted to make a suitable return for it all. So, she endeavored to amuse him with cheerful chat, music, and reading aloud anything that he seemed to care to hear.

He fell more deeply in love with her day by day, and he often found it difficult to refrain from telling the tale to her and pleading for a return. His mother saw it all, and at length she advised him to speak to Gracie's father, tell him the whole story, and gain permission to tell of his love and say what he could to win her heart.

"I have thought it might be best to wait some years, mother," he said. "I fear he will be too greatly astonished and indignant, and then he may deprive me of her sweet society."

"Astonished he probably will be," she said, "but surely not indignant. When he has fully considered the matter, remembering that there is no blood tie between you, I think he will not withhold his consent—provided you are willing to defer marriage till she is of suitable age."

"I hope you are right, mother, but such a mixture of relationships as it would make. I fear he will think that an insurmountable difficulty."

"But to rob his dearly loved daughter of a life of wedded happiness he will think still worse, if I am not greatly mistaken in him. And as for the mixture of relationships, you can still be brother to him and your sister Violet, and Gracie remain his daughter."

"You are the best of comforters and advisers, mother," he said, "and I will take your advice and make a clean breast of it to the captain at the earliest opportunity."

He did so before the day was over. Seeing the captain in the grounds, he joined him with a request for a bit of a private chat.

"Certainly," said the captain, leading the way to the summerhouse on the edge of the cliff. "If you want assistance in any way that I can give it, I need hardly tell you that it will be a pleasure to me to do so—especially as you are the brother of my dear wife."

"Thank you, Brother Levis, I do not doubt that in the least, and yet—" he stammered and paused, coloring deeply.

"I think you need not hesitate to tell me," the captain said with a look of surprise. "I feel very sure you would not ask anything wrong or unreasonable of me."

"No. My request is neither, I think. It is that I may, if I can, win the heart and hand of your daughter Gracie."

"Surely, surely, you must acknowledge that that is unreasonable!" exclaimed the captain in a tone of astonishment not unmixed with indignation. "Such a mixture of relationships—making you your sister's son-in-law and my daughter my sister-in-law!"

"My mother's idea is that we might keep to our own relationships as they are now. She thinks as there is absolutely no tie of blood between us, there could be nothing wrong in such a marriage."

"No, perhaps not absolutely wrong, but it is still very distasteful to me. Besides, as you yourself must acknowledge, Gracie is entirely too young to marry."

"But all the time growing older, as well as more and more beautiful, and I can wait. She is worth waiting for as long as Jacob served for Rachel. And would it not be wise to give her to a physician, who will make her health his constant care?"

"Perhaps so," returned the captain with a rather perplexed and sad sort of smile. "If you have won her heart and are willing to wait till she is of suitable age, I—don't forbid you to tell her how dearly you love her—if you can."

"A thousand thanks, Brother Levis!" exclaimed Harold, seizing the captain's hand in a vise-like grasp and giving it a hearty shake.

"I don't know how to put my love into words—it seems to me they would be powerless to express it—but I shall try and hope to win a return by untiring devotion."

"She has a loving heart, and her father finds it hard to be called upon to resign the first place in it," the captain said with an involuntary sigh.

"Let us hope that it will be for her happiness, captain. I think we both love her well enough to resign a good deal for that."

"Her father certainly does," said the captain. "Dear child! She has been a great comfort and blessing to me since my eyes first rested upon her dear little face. She has never caused me a pang, except by her ill-health and feebleness."

"I have known her long enough and well enough to be sure of that," said Harold. "She certainly has a lovely disposition, as well as a beautiful face and form. I feel that to win her for my own will be the greatest good fortune that could possibly come to me."

"I am glad you appreciate the worth of my dear child," the captain said with emotion. "If you have won her heart, I am not afraid to trust her happiness to your keeping. But, understand, I cannot let you take her at once."

"Yes, I understand, and I shall not take any unfair advantage of your reluctantly granted permission, Brother Levis. But if I can win her consent, her heart, I shall be a very happy man and wait contentedly—or at least ungrumblingly—until you grant us leave to become man and wife at last."

Harold was not long in availing himself of the consent given. He was on the watch for an opportunity to tell his tale of love to the one most deeply concerned. He coaxed her out to that very spot where he and her father had had their private talk, there told her what she was to him, and asked if she could return his affection and willingly give herself to him. She was evidently much surprised, listened with an agitated air and face suffused with blushes, and then said low and hesitatingly, "Oh, Uncle Harold! How can you? You are so good and wise—so much older than I am—and—and father has often told me that I am only a little girl—not nearly old enough to think about—about such things—and so I am sure he wouldn't want you to talk to me as you did just now."

"But I spoke to him first, and I have gained his permission to tell you of my love. He probably will not let us marry for some years to come, even if you care for me in that way. But he is willing that we should become engaged if we choose and court until he thinks you are old enough to marry. Oh, darling, if you care for me and will promise to be mine some day, it will make me the happiest of men! Oh, dearest! Can't you love me in that way, even just a little?" he concluded inquiringly, taking her hand in his and holding it in a tenderly affectionate pressure.

"I can't help loving you, Uncle Harold. You are so, so very good and kind to me. But I never thought of—of your being my suitor. I'm not wise and good enough for you."

"I should put it just the other way, that I am not half wise and good enough for you, my darling, my fairy queen," he said, venturing to put an arm about her, draw her into a close embrace, and press an ardent kiss upon her lips.

She made no resistance to his advance, and a few more words of love and whispered tenderness caused the sweet, blushing face to grow radiant with happiness. She did not deny that she returned his affection, and at length she owned in a few low-breathed, hesitating words that she did.

Her face was beaming when they returned to the house, and when she came to her father for the usual goodnight caress, he folded her close to his heart. He gazed searchingly into the sweet, blushing face and said tenderly, "My darling little daughter looks very happy tonight. Won't you let your father into the secret of it?"

"Yes, indeed, papa. I never meant to keep anything from you," she murmured, half under her breath, hiding her fair, blushing face on his shoulder. "I always mean to tell you everything worthwhile, because we love each other so very, very much. I am happy because of what Uncle Harold has been telling me. He says he told you first, so you know. You are willing, then, papa?"

"Yes, daughter, when the right time comes, since it seems it will make you happy. But," he sighed, "it is a little hard for your father to find other men getting the love of his dear daughters away from him."

"Oh, papa. Dear, dearest papa, don't think that!" she said with tears in her voice. "I've always loved you dearly, and it seems to me that I love you better just now than I ever did before."

"Ah, is that so, daughter mine?" he said, giving her another tender caress. "It makes me happy to hear it and to believe that my dear Gracie will never cease to love me and will always feel sure of her father's loving sympathy in all her joys and sorrows."

"It is very sweet to know that, papa dear," she said. "Oh, I am just the happiest girl with so many and such dear loved ones. But even with all the others, father, I couldn't do without your love."

"I hope not, dear child. It would be hard indeed for me to doubt that or to be deprived of yours. But now bid me goodnight and go to your rest, for late hours have always been very bad for you."

"Yes, sir, I know. And my dear, kind father is always so tenderly careful of me," she said, giving and receiving a close, loving embrace.

It had been a sultry day followed by quite a delightful evening, a cool, refreshing breeze coming from the river and a full moon in a clear sky making it almost as light as day in the grounds, about which the elder members of the party were scattered. The captain left the porch where he and his daughter Gracie had had their little chat and joined a group under the trees on the lawn. It consisted of Mrs. Travilla — or Grandma Elsie, as his first set of children had been accustomed to call her — her daughters, Mrs. Leland and Mrs. Raymond, and her sons Harold, Herbert, and Walter. There was a slight flutter of excitement among them as he joined them and took possession of a vacant seat.

"I am glad you have come, captain," said Mrs. Travilla. "Harold has been telling us of your great kindness to him, and I want to thank you for it."

"Ah! What was that?" he asked in a tone that seemed to express surprise. "There are few things I would not do for you or yours, mother."

"I believe that, and you have given him the right to win, if he can, a precious treasure and to give me the dearest of little daughters."

"Ah, yes!" he said, as if just comprehending her meaning. "To her father, she is such a treasure as any might covet and be rejoiced to win."

"An opinion in which I am sure we will all agree," said Violet. "I, who certainly know her well, think she is an inestimable treasure."

"An opinion in which we can all join you, I am sure," added Herbert. "I think my brother is a most fortunate man."

"That is exactly what he thinks of himself," said Harold with a happy laugh. "Though there has to be a long, long waiting spell before the full extent of that happiness can be realized."

"How our young folks are pairing off!" remarked Mrs. Leland with a slight sigh.

"Ah, yes," said Violet. "Fortunately, they don't pair off with strangers and leave us. That makes it easier to bear. Doesn't it, my dear?"

"Yes, except for the mixture of relationships," returned the captain a trifle ruefully.

"Is it to be kept a secret?" queried Mrs. Leland.

"I am certainly willing it should be known in the connection," said Captain Raymond.

CHAPTER THIRTEENTH

IT WAS GROWING quite late, and Evelyn's guests, accustomed to keeping early hours while at Crag Cottage, had nearly all retired to their rooms for the night. But Chester Dinsmore and Lucilla Raymond were just returning from a stroll down the riverbank, and as they neared the house, they could see the captain pacing the front porch.

"There is papa now," said Lucilla. "I am afraid he will think I have been out rather late."

"Are you afraid of a scolding?" asked Chester.

"No. I may get a gentle reproof but nothing worse. Papa never really scolds, but I can't bear to have him displeased with me. My dear, dear father! I believe I give him all the love that would have been divided between him and my mother had she lived."

"I am not surprised at that," returned Chester, "for he is certainly worthy of it. I have learned to love and honor him myself as if I were his own son."

"Oh, Chester, how glad I am to hear you say that!" exclaimed Lucilla.

But that ended the talk for they were at the foot of the porch steps, and the captain spoke, addressing them. "Ah, so here you are at last, my dears. I was beginning to feel a trifle anxious lest something had befallen you."

"Oh, no, father! We are all right," exclaimed Lucilla in lively tones. "But the bewitching moonlight and pleasant breeze tempted us to linger longer than usual. I hope you are not vexed with us?"

"Not very seriously, daughter," he said with a smile, "but it is high time now that you were getting ready for your night's rest. I want you to have plenty of that, and I know you like to be up early."

"Yes, indeed, father. My early walks and talks with you are among my greatest pleasures."

"Your father in the morning, your fiancé at night," Chester said with a pleasant laugh. "I'm glad and thankful, captain, that you let me have her for something like half the time. Goodnight, now! And pleasant dreams to you both," he added, turning away and passing into the house, hardly waiting for their return of his parting good wishes.

"Now I suppose I must say goodnight and go, too," Lucilla said, putting her arms about her father's neck and looking lovingly into his face.

"I shall take about five minutes of your society first," he returned, smiling and patting her cheek. "I have something to tell you—something that will, perhaps, be a little surprise to you."

"Nothing bad, I hope, father?"

"No, not exactly bad—though I must own it is something of a trial to me. Your sister Gracie has followed your bad example and given the first place in her heart to another. My consent has been asked, given, and they are engaged, though not to marry for the next five years."

"Father!" exclaimed Lucilla in a tone of utter astonishment. "To whom? Can it be Chester's brother Frank?"

"What a guess!" laughed her father. "No. Try again, Lu."

She reflected a moment. "It can't be Uncle Harold?" she ventured in a tone that seemed to say that it was hardly possible. "He is surely much too old for her."

"Unfortunately I cannot make that objection, since there is some years less difference in their ages than in your Mamma Vi's and mine."

"Oh, papa! And are they really lovers, and they are engaged?"

"Yes. Though such a match is in ways very distasteful to me—simply on account of the mixed-up relationships with family members that their marriage would bring about. But when I found the fancy and affection was mutual, I could not withhold my consent."

"You, dear father! You are always so kindly considerate of other people's welfare and happiness," she said in tones tremulous with emotion. "I am sure nobody ever had a kinder, better father than ours."

"It is most pleasant to have my daughter think so, whether I deserve it or not," he said low and tenderly, holding her close to his heart and pressing kisses on her forehead and cheek. "Now go and make yourself ready for bed," he added, "and don't let this bit of surprising news keep you from sleeping. I want my eldest daughter fresh and bright for my entertainment in the morning."

The house being so full, Lucilla, Gracie, and Evelyn shared the same room. Gracie was in bed, but she was not asleep as usual, and Eva was preparing for rest when Lucilla came in from her talk with her father. She glanced at her sister, and seeing her eyes closed, thought her sleeping.

"Oh, Eva!" she whispered to her friend. "Do you know? Have you heard the news?"

"News? No. I have been busy about household matters, and no one has told anything. What is it—war news?"

"No, oh, no!" glancing smilingly toward Gracie, "something even more interesting, I think, unless Max were concerned in it. It is that we have another pair of lovers in the house— Gracie there and Uncle Harold. I'll have to quit calling him 'uncle,' though since he is to be my brother one of these days."

"Is it possible?! Well, he has won a very great prize, I think."

Gracie was not asleep now. Her eyes, wide open, were fixed on the two girls, and her cheeks were rosy with blushes. "No, it's I that have,

Eva," she said. "I don't know how anybody so good and wise and kind could take a fancy to poor, silly, little me!"

At that, Lucilla ran to the bed, threw her arms about her sister, and showered her with kisses upon her lips and cheeks. "You dear, dear thing! You are neither poor nor silly," she said. "I think the only wonder is that all the men don't fall head over ears in love with you. They certainly would if they had good sense, taste, and discernment."

At that, Gracie indulged in a peal of low, soft laughter. "You funny girl!" she said. "I am glad indeed that they are not so silly, for what in the world could I do with so many love interests? One is quite a plentiful supply for me."

"That's right, Gracie," exclaimed Evelyn. "I'm sure one such as mine should be quite enough for anybody as well."

"Well, I'm not going to say 'Uncle Harold' any more," laughed Lucilla.

"No, he doesn't want either of us to," said Gracie. "But now I suppose both he and papa would say I must try to go at once to sleep."

"Ye. So I'll stop hugging and kissing you and be quiet as a mouse, getting ready for bed, so as not to keep you awake," said Lucilla, giving her little sister a final loving embrace and gliding away from the bed to the dressing table to make her own preparations for bed.

"Do you think Max will like it?" asked Gracie in an undertone.

"Yes, I do. He and Harold have always been good friends. But as papa says, it will make an unpleasant mixture of relationships. He will be brother-in-law to Gracie besides being her own father," she added with a slight laugh. "Yet I know very well she will always remember that he is her father — her dearly loved and honored father."

"I am certain of it," said Evelyn. "She would never make the match without her father's knowledge and consent."

"No, indeed!" responded Lucilla, turning a loving look upon the now sleeping Gracie.

Lucilla had scarcely left her father on the porch when Violet joined him there.

"I thought it possible, Levis, that you might not object to your wife's company in your walk here," she said in a lively tone, slipping her hand into his arm.

"Object, my darling, light of my eyes and joy of my heart!" he said in a loving, mirthful tone, bending down to kiss the sweet lips. "Yours is the sweetest companionship I know of. I should be glad to think mine was as delightful to you."

"As I don't know how to measure either one, I can only say that it is the most delightful of all in the world to me," she returned with a happy laugh. Then in a somewhat graver tone, "Oh, my dear husband, you don't know how dearly I and all your children love you! Neither Elsie nor Ned is willing to go to bed without your fatherly goodnight caresses, and they always bewail the necessity for doing so when you are away from home."

"Probably not regretting it more than their father does," he said. "Yes, the love of my children is a highly esteemed blessing to me, and, unfortunately, I cannot help feeling it something of a grief and disappointment when I learn that their tenderest affection has been transferred to another."

"Ah, you are thinking of Gracie and Harold. But be comforted, my dear. I am certain that Gracie does not love her father less because Harold has won a place in her heart. I do not love my dear mother any less for loving you, my dear husband, or you any the less for loving her."

"I am glad to hear it, my darling," he said, tenderly pressing the hand she had laid in his.

"And surely we cannot blame my brother and your daughter for loving each other when they are both so worthy of affection that no one who knows them can help giving it to them."

"You are a special pleader, my dear," he said with a smile. "They hardly need one with me, for I am fond of them both—particularly my frail young daughter."

"Ah, and does that not cause you to rejoice that she loves, and is loved by, a good and successful physician, who can care for her?"

"That is a cause for thankfulness, my dear," he returned pleasantly. "But shall we not go in now and retire to rest? It is growing late."

"Yes, if you have finished your promenade. I don't want to rob you of that."

"I think I have taken sufficient exercise, and I now prefer rest and sleep," he answered lightly, as he drew her on toward the doorway.

As Lucilla came tripping down the stairway the next morning, Harold was passing through the lower hall.

"Good morning, Lu," he said, looking at her.

"Good morning, Dr. Travilla," she returned rather demurely.

"What!" he exclaimed. "What's that you are calling me?"

"Dr. Travilla. That's your name. Isn't it?"

"Yes—to strangers and people not related to me, but—you called me 'uncle' yesterday.

"But you're not my uncle, and it seems you intend to become my brother-in-law, so—"

"So Harold without the 'uncle' would be the most appropriate name. Wouldn't it?"

"Perhaps so, if—if you won't think it in any way disrespectful."

"Not a bit of it. Call me Harold, or I'll be very apt to call you Mrs. Dinsmore one of these days."

They ended with a laugh and a very cordial handshaking, just as the captain appeared in the outer doorway. Then they joined him in a stroll about the grounds.

"There is a dark cloud in the east," remarked Lucilla in a regretful tone. "We are likely to have a rainy day. Are we not, papa?"

"Yes," he said, "but it need not necessarily be an unpleasant one. We may find plenty of indoor employment and recreations."

"Yes," said Harold. "There have been many pleasant rainy days in my past experiences. And they are not so bad for a strong, healthy man, even if he must go out in the rain."

"And when gardens and fields are needing rain, we long and pray for it," added Lucilla.

"How is Gracie this morning?" asked Harold.

"She was still sleeping when I left the room," replied Lucilla. "But probably she is up and ready for the call to breakfast by this time."

"And there it is," said the captain, as the sound of the ringing of the hand bell came from the house. "So let us go in and not keep the others waiting for breakfast."

They met Violet and Gracie in the hall as they entered, and it was pretty to see the latter's blush and smile as Harold greeted her.

The clouds were increasing in the sky and growing darker, and before they left the table, the rain had begun to fall. So they talked of indoor occupations and amusements.

"We might have a little fun, if everybody's willing," remarked Ned Raymond, giving Mr. Lilburn a significant look and smile.

"Yes. Little boys—big ones, too—can generally get up some fun among themselves when they try," was Cousin Ronald's answering remark without any indication that he took Ned's hint.

"And I know Cousin Ronald is very kind about helping in that," returned Ned insinuatingly.

"Yes, he is fond of giving pleasure to his young friends," remarked Mrs. Lilburn with a loving smile up into her husband's face. "I think, Ned, he will help you to some before the day is over."

They were on the porch, for there was no wind at the moment to drive the rain in upon them, and it was cooler there than within doors. As Annis finished speaking, there was a sudden cry of distress, seemingly coming from the river just below. "Help! Help! I shall drown! Nobody will help me!"

It was a man's voice, and there was a foreign accent in the tones. It made quite a stir in the little assembly on the porch, the lads exclaiming: "Oh, the poor fellow! Can't we help him, Grandma Elsie? Surely the men on the *Dolphin* will do what they can!"

But hardly were the words spoken, when another voice called out in reply to the first, "Hold on there, me jewel, an' I'll give ye a lift. I'm the b'ye that kin do it."

"Oh, I hope he will get him out!" cried Ned in great excitement. "Papa, you'll let them take him on board the yacht. Won't you?"

"Certainly, if he wishes to be taken there," replied the captain with a smiling glance at Cousin Ronald.

Just then the second voice called out, "Here he is—the half drownded Frenchman. An' now will the likes of yees aboord that craft take 'im in an' dry 'im off?"

"Of course. That's exactly what the captain would do if he were here," answered a third voice, which sounded exactly like that of the man at present in charge of the yacht.

"Oh, I'm glad he didn't drown!" exclaimed Elsie Raymond with a sigh of relief.

"I presume such people don't often drown, Elsie dear," laughed her mother.

"Oh, mamma, I often hear stories of people drowning," said the little girl. "And, Uncle Harold, don't they need a doctor when they are nearly drowned?"

"They are very apt to," he replied with a slight laugh. "Do you want me to go down now and see about that man?"

"If you could, without getting wet," she answered hesitatingly.

"Suppose I go," said her Uncle Herbert. "I'm pretty well now and am perhaps almost as skillful a physician as my older brother."

But now the captain interposed.

"I can't let either of my young brothers expose himself to this rain, for the men on yacht are quite competent to deal with that Frenchman's case and needs."

"I should say so, indeed," said Mr. Lilburn gravely. "It is not likely that he was in the water many minutes. So, my wee bonny bairnie Elsie, dinna fash yersel' ony mair aboot him," he concluded with an affectionate look and smile into the face of the little girl.

"Oh, Cousin Ronald, did you do it all?" exclaimed Ned. "Dear me, how stupid I am! I might have known it was you."

"I doubt if you really know it yet, laddie," laughed the old gentleman.

Ned turned to his father. "Papa, may I take an umbrella and just run down to the *Dolphin* for a few minutes to ask about it?"

"It is not worth while," replied the captain. "I am very sure you would make no discoveries."

"Then it was you, Cousin Ronald. Wasn't it, now? Please own up," exclaimed Ned with a laughing look into the old gentleman's face.

"Folk shouldna find any kinda fault with what they've asked for," was the old gentleman's noncommittal rejoinder.

"Oh, no, sir! No, indeed! But I was not meaning to find fault," laughed Ned. "I think it was good fun, and I hope you will give us some more of it."

Just as he pronounced the last word, a fierce bark, seemingly that of a very large dog, followed instantly by a scream as if a woman were in pain and terror, startled them all. Then there were outcries of affright from the children, while several of the grown people started to their feet and looked anxiously in the direction of the sounds, which had seemed to come from the vicinity of the porch but a little farther toward the rear of the house.

Another bark from the dog, then a woman's voice in tones of wild affright, "Oh, somebody help! Help! This dog will tear me to pieces."

Mr. Leland and Walter Travilla stepped quite quickly to the end of the porch nearest the sounds and looked around the corner of the house, but they instantly reported that neither woman nor dog was to be seen.

"Oh, another sell from Cousin Ronald!" laughed Ned. "Oh, there it is again!" for just then there was a sound as of a loud knock at a side door, and a man's coarse voice thundering, "Let me in oot o' this rain, ye slow-going, good-for-naughthins. Let me in, I say, and be right quick about it."

A woman's scream followed instantly, "Oh, captain or some o' you gentlemen, come here quick and save us from this drunken rascal."

Some of those on the porch were a little startled for an instant, but a laugh quickly followed. The fun went on for some minutes — bees, mice, chickens, and puppies being heard but not seen or felt.

But the rainfall was growing heavier, and at length Harold suggested that it might be well for Gracie, if not for all, to go within doors to escape the dampness.

Nearly all complied with the suggestion, and Mrs. Travilla, inviting Gracie to a seat by her side, said low and tenderly, "Harold gave me a piece of news last night that has made me very happy. I hope one of these days to number you among my dear daughters, and I shall feel most happy in doing so."

"Oh, Grandma Elsie, it is so kind in you to say that!" returned Gracie tremulously but blushing with pleasure as she spoke. "It will be very sweet to have you for my mother, for I have loved you dearly ever since I first saw you."

At that moment Walter came and took a seat on the other side of her.

"Oh, Gracie," he said in an undertone, "I am so glad of Harold's news — that I am to have you for a sister at some future day. I'll try to be a good brother to you."

"And I certainly intend to do my best to be a good sister to you, Walter," she answered in the same low tone and with a vivid blush and one of her sweetest smiles.

"Thanks," he said. "I wish the wedding was to take place directly — some time this fall, at least. Couldn't we coax your father to allow it?"

She laughed and shook her head. "Papa would never allow it, and I — don't believe I could consent myself. Really, the very thought of doing anything so important so suddenly more than half frightens me."

"Harold is a mild, good-natured kind of fellow. You needn't be afraid of him," laughed Walter.

"No, not of him exactly," returned Gracie, laughing a little also and blushing quite a good deal, "but of — of the sudden change in my way of life—of leaving my father and all the rest of my family."

But there the talk between them ended for the time, for Harold's near relatives came up, one after another, to tell Gracie how welcome a new member of their near connection she would be. Chester was the only one who expressed any regret, and that not to Gracie but to Lucilla.

"I am sorry for my brother Frank," he said. "He has been desperately in love with her, but your father would not let him speak. And I thought it would be pleasant to be so closely and doubly connected—two sisters marrying brothers."

"I am sorry, since it disappoints you," said Lucilla. "But I hope Frank will soon get over his disappointment and find someone who will suit him still better. Besides, Gracie being so delicate, it is well for her to get into the hands of a good physician."

"True enough," returned Chester. "And we may as well look at it in that way, for there is no use fretting over what can't be helped."

𝕩 𝕩 𝕩 𝕩 𝕩

September had come. The summer heat was over, and business called the gentlemen of the party to their more southern homes. Preparations began, and one little company after another departed, leaving the rest feeling somewhat lonely and dull without them. The captain and his family, Grandma Elsie, Evelyn, and Mr. and Mrs. Lilburn were to go in the yacht, which carried them away a few days later—down the Hudson River and down the Atlantic coast to the seaport near their Southern homes.

A joyous welcome from relatives and friends awaited them there. Then followed the fall, winter, and early spring months filled up and made delightful by the accustomed round of study, needlework, social calls, and visits interspersed with religious duties and charitable work.

Evelyn was often at Woodburn, and she and Lucilla made many pretty things for the adornment of their future homes. The weddings were to be postponed till Max came home, and to their disappointment that homecoming was deferred month after month until Chester grew exceedingly weary of the waiting. Letters were received occasionally from Max, but he knew no more than they when he would be able to rejoin them and claim his bonny bride. The waiting was doubtless harder for him than for Chester or either of the girls. They indeed seemed to take it quietly and contentedly.

Gracie was very happy with her suitor close at hand and often visiting her professionally or otherwise. And with her, this state of things seemed to be conducive to her health. She grew rosier, stronger, merrier, and more lively in her speech and manner than she had ever been before. So great a joy was it to her father to perceive the change, that he soon fully forgave Harold for seeking her affection while she was still so young and feeble. Harold seemed to be waiting very patiently, and when Chester grumbled at his long enforced wait, Lucilla sometimes playfully called his attention to the good example set him by Harold.

"But there isn't the same need of waiting in our case," he would reply. "For, I am thankful to say, you are as healthy a girl as any that I know of."

"Yes, but think of the disappointment to Max and Eva if we shouldn't wait for them, when we can be together almost as much as if we were married. All the time, we can do things to make our new home as lovely as possible."

The continuance of the war in the Philippines, a cause of more or less regret to everybody, was doubly so to Max's friends and relatives, because it delayed his return month after month. They missed him particularly when Christmas time came, and he was not there to share in the pleasant exchange of gifts and greetings. They had sent gifts to him, hoping they would reach him in good season, and as usual they bestowed them upon each other. For weeks beforehand Violet had spent a good deal of time in her studio, and the result was a handsome portrait of the captain for each of his older daughters. They were highly pleased with them, saying that nothing else could have given them so much pleasure. The captain's gifts to them and Violet were valuable books and some fine paintings for their walls.

"You see, Chester," Lucilla said, when exhibiting hers to him, "that we are getting more and more for the adornment of our home while we wait for it."

"Adornment that could go on just as well if we were already in it," he returned with a rather rueful laugh.

"Well, for your consolation please remember that it is near enough to be looked at every day," replied Lucilla in a sprightly tone. "And see here what your fiancée has prepared for you," drawing a small package from her pocket as she spoke.

"Thanks! Some of her own work, I hope," he said with a gratified look and smile.

"Yes, I would have you enjoy as much of my work as possible."

He had it opened now and found a beaded purse.

"Oh, how handsome!" he cried. "Many, many thanks, dearest! I have no need of a reminder of you, but if I had, this would be one every time I looked at it. Now here is my gift to you," taking in his turn a little package from his pocket and putting it in her hand. It was a miniature of himself — a fine likeness — attached to a beautiful gold chain.

"Oh, it is excellent, and nothing could have pleased me better!" she exclaimed, as she closely examined it.

Harold had the same sort of gift for Gracie, and she had embroidered for him a set of fine linen cambric handkerchiefs with which he seemed greatly pleased.

Every member of that family and each of the others in the connection had prepared some gift of value for each of the others, for their servants and dependents, and for the neighbors who were in need of assistance from those able to give it.

As usual, there was a grand dinner at Ion, to which all the connection were invited. Pretty much the same thing was repeated at Woodburn on New Year's Day. Max was missed and talked of at both gatherings, always being mentioned as one of whom they were proud and fond, while to Evelyn and the Woodburn family his absence detracted much from the enjoyment of the festivities. Yet they comforted themselves with the hope that the trouble in the Philippines would soon be over and he be allowed to return to his home and dear ones, now so anxious to see him, and to claim his promised wife.

CHAPTER
FOURTEENTH

THE WINTER QUIETLY passed away without any untoward event to the friends at Woodburn, Ion, Fairview, and the vicinity. March and April succeeded, then early in May came the news that Admiral Watson was ordered to proceed to Manila and relieve Admiral Dewey. He sailed from San Francisco on the sixteenth. It was not until late in June that he had reached his destination, but Admiral Dewey had left there for Hong Kong on the twenty-third of May and placed the *Olympia* in dry dock for the ten days he thought best to stay at that point in order to recruit his own health and that of his men. He left Hong Kong on June the sixth and reached Singapore on June the eleventh. On the twenty-third, he was at Colombo on the island of Ceylon. He touched at various points on his homeward route—Port Said, Trieste, Naples, Leghorn, at every place being received with highest honors. On August twenty-eighth, he was in the neighborhood of Nice and Villefranche, enjoying the delightful climate and beautiful scenery of that part of the world. On the fourth of September, he reached Gibraltar. His vessel gave the usual salute, heartily acknowledged by the garrison, and the admiral was warmly welcomed by its commander-in-chief, General Biddulph. It would seem he stayed there six days, as it was on the tenth he sailed for New York by way of the Azores. On Tuesday morning of September the twenty-sixth, he anchored inside Sandy Hook—three days earlier than he was expected.

A reception committee in New York City had been busily making ready to give him a grand "Welcome Home," which they intended should eclipse in gorgeous pageantry everything that had preceded it in the way of public demonstration. They had written to Admiral Dewey to know when he would arrive in order that they might fix a date for the grand display, and he had written them from Leghorn, more than a month before. "I shall, without fail, reach the Lower Bay on Friday, September twenty-ninth."

The glad news of his arrival quickly spread by telegraph, and cannon were fired and bells rung in many cities throughout the country. The New York Reception Committee hastened to welcome him as soon as they knew of the arrival of the *Olympia*. Rear-Admirals Philip and Sampson came also, but first of all came Sir Thomas Lipton, the British challenger for the cup which has been so long in our possession, his vessel lying near where the *Olympia* anchored.

But presently another yacht came steaming rapidly down the river, and Max recognized it with an exclamation of delight, for it was the *Dolphin*. In a few minutes more Captain Raymond was on the deck of the *Olympia*, grasping his son's hand, while his eyes shone with fatherly pride and affection.

"My boy, my dear boy!" he said in tones tremulous with emotion. "Thank God that we are permitted to meet again."

"Father, my dear, dear father, how I have longed for this meeting with you!" was Max's answering exclamation. "Oh, tell me, are all our dear ones alive and well?"

"Yes, my son, and waiting yonder in the yacht for you. Surely the admiral will allow you to go aboard her with me for a little visit."

The admiral and the captain were not strangers to each other. A cordial greeting passed between them. They chatted as old friends for a few minutes, but then Captain Raymond carried his son off to the *Dolphin*, where he was received most joyfully. He exchanged loving embraces with his affianced, his sisters, "Mamma Vi," "Grandma Elsie," and his little brother.

They told him they had spent the greater part of the summer at Crag Cottage, which they still considered their temporary home. But for the present they were on board their floating home, as the best place from which to glimpse a view the naval welcome for Admiral Dewey and his gallant crew.

Time flew fast in the glad mutual interaction they had lacked for so many months. Max had many questions to ask in regard to friends and relatives and all that had been going on in the neighborhood of his home and theirs. But his short leave had soon expired, and his father conveyed him back to the *Olympia* and left him there with the warmly expressed hope that they would soon be able to be together constantly for a time.

At the naval anchorage at Tompkinsville, a fleet was gathered to welcome Dewey's return, and his vessel steamed thither on Wednesday — the day after her arrival at Sandy Hook. As she swept up the bay, the salute due to an Admiral of the United States Navy rang out over the harbor from the forts and the assembled fleet for the first time in many years. There were also the music of marine bands, the pealing of naval bugles, the shrill whistles of numerous small craft, the cheering of excursion parties, and the rapid dash of the steam launches, all combining to make the scene a lively one.

During that day and the next, the admiral and his officers had little rest, for their time was devoted to receiving the hurried visits of state and city officials, of naval and military officers, and of thousands of private citizens. One of the calls was that of a committee from Washington to tell Dewey of the arrangements for his reception, the sword presentation there, and of an invitation to dine with President McKinley on October third.

On Thursday, Captain Lamberton of the *Olympia* had a pleasant task—that of pinning upon the chest of each man of Dewey's fleet who had taken part in the fight for Manila the bronze medal of honor voted him by Congress. That was followed by the presentation to Admiral Dewey of the first American admiral's flag ever flung to the breeze—the flag first hoisted to the mast-head of Farragut's flagship, the *Hartford*, before New Orleans.

Another thing very pleasing to the admiral was the receipt of an order from Washington granting special permission to the thirty-four Chinamen on board the *Olympia* who had taken part in the battle at Manila to land and have a share in the great parade. The city was a blaze of flags and bunting by day and of electric lights by night. On the Brooklyn Bridge over eight thousand electric bulbs were arranged to form the words "Welcome Dewey." Very powerful searchlights flashed from the towers over city and bay, and red fire burned from along the shores upon the vessels at night.

The naval parade on Friday was the most magnificent display of its kind ever seen in this country. The *Olympia* led the way, followed by battleships, cruisers, revenue cutters, torpedo boats, and innumerable craft of all descriptions. Over three million people lined the riverbanks to see the magnificent pageant. At Riverside—where Grant is buried—a salute was fired in his honor. Two beautiful allegorical floats were anchored there, representing "Victory" and "Peace." Here the *Olympia* and her consorts dropped anchor, while the long fleet passed in review. In the evening, there was a fine electric and pyrotechnic display throughout the city and along the river.

The next day, Saturday, September thirtieth, came the land parade, which was as interesting as had been the naval one. At five o'clock, the admiral was up, and personally inspected his men. A committee of gentlemen escorted him to City Hall, where he was met by Admiral Schley, Captain Walker, Captain Cogland, Captain Dyer, Governor Roosevelt, and others who had won distinction in the war. It was observed that he greeted Schley with marked cordiality. From there, the party went to a stand in front of the Hall, and Dewey was presented by Mayor Van Wyck on behalf of the City of New York with a handsome and costly loving cup of fine gold.

The admiral and his party then hastened to the pier to take the boat to Grant's tomb, where the procession formed. It was a great one, and every step of the way was an ovation. First came Sousa's immense band of musicians, then the sailor boys of Manila, the blue-jackets of Santiago, and the boys from fifteen states who had all taken part in the Spanish-American War. The immense crowds along the sidewalks cheered them lustily—none more so than the "Fighting Tenth" of Pennsylvania.

But the part of the procession that attracted the most attention was the carriage drawn by four beautiful bay horses in which rode Admiral Dewey and Mayor Van Wyck. Dewey rode with uncovered head bowing right and left until he reached the reviewing stand. The triumphal arch with its marble-like colonnade made a beautiful picture. On its top was a heroic figure of Farragut—who gave Dewey his first lesson in sailing over hidden mines and destructive torpedoes—seeming to look down upon his brave and successful pupil with admiration and approval. The celebration was a great success, showing how heartily the American people appreciated their gallant hero. The next day, being the Sabbath, was spent in rest and comparative quiet. On Monday, October second, Dewey went by rail from New York to Washington, his journey thither proving a continual ovation. It was in the early evening he reached that city, and as the train neared the station, a battery boomed out the admiral's salute, announcing his arrival to the waiting multitudes. The Third Cavalry was there to receive him, and he was driven to the White House to pay his respects to the Chief of the Nation. He was warmly welcomed by the President and his Cabinet and many naval officers.

After that, the entire party went to review the civic parade that had been planned in honor of Admiral Dewey.

The next day, Admiral Dewey was presented with the sword voted him by Congress. A vast concourse of people assembled to witness the imposing and impressive ceremony, which took place in front of the Capitol in the presence of the President and his Cabinet and the principal officers of several departments of the government. General Miles was grand marshal of the escort attended by a large staff of officers of the army and navy all in full dress uniform and superbly mounted.

Just as the meridian gun sounded high noon, Admiral Dewey, leaning upon the President's arm, walked upon the platform. Following them were judges of the Supreme Court, governors of states, senators, members of Congress, and the general officers of the army and navy.

Congress had directed that the sword should be presented by the Secretary of the Navy, and he did so in most appropriate and eloquent language and ceremony.

"No captain," he said, "ever faced a more crucial test than when, that morning, bearing the fate and honor of your country in your hand, thousands of miles from home with every foreign port in the world shut to you, nothing between you and annihilation but the thin sheathing of your ships, your cannon, and your devoted officers and men, you moved upon the enemy's batteries on shore and on sea with unflinching faith and nerve and before the sun was halfway up in the heavens, had silenced the guns of the foe, sunk the hostile fleet, demonstrated the supremacy of American sea power, and transferred to the United States an empire of the islands of the Pacific."

In closing his speech, the Secretary handed the sword to the President as Commander-in-Chief of the Army and Navy, and the President, speaking a few appropriate words as he did so, handed it to the admiral, who took it, saying, "I thank you, Mr. President, for this great honor you have conferred upon me. I thank the Congress for what it has done. I thank the Secretary of the Navy for his gracious words. I thank my country for this beautiful gift, which shall be an heirloom in my family forever, as an evidence that republics are not ungrateful. And I thank you, Mr. Chairman and gentlemen of the committee, for the gracious, kindly, and cordial welcome, which you have given me to my home."

CHAPTER FIFTEENTH

IT WAS A LOVELY evening, and a pleasant company had gathered upon the deck of the *Dolphin*, Captain Raymond's yacht. She was lying in New York harbor, and there were Mrs. Travilla, or Grandma Elsie, as some of her loved ones called her, Captain Raymond himself, his wife and children, older and younger, Evelyn Leland, Dr. Harold Travilla, and Chester Dinsmore. They were scattered in groups—the three pairs of lovers in one, and they were conversing in low, earnest tones, now and then varied by a ripple of laugher.

"I should like it very, very much," said Eva. "But I doubt if the captain will prove willing."

"If he consulted only his own inclination, Eva, he would not consent," said Max. "But father is anything else but selfish, and he loves you so dearly, my sweet, that I by no means despair of persuading him to give you your wish in regard to this."

"I have hardly a doubt of that," said Lucilla. "I am now highly in favor of the plan, though I was not at first."

"It suits me exactly," remarked Chester in a gleeful tone. "I greatly like the idea of taking my wife home with me."

"Something that more than one of us would be glad to do," sighed Harold, squeezing affectionately a little, white hand of which he had taken possession a moment before.

"Never mind, old fellow, your turn will come one of these days, I hope," said Chester. "Perhaps when you two have waited as long as Lu and I have now."

"Ah, I'm afraid we have even a longer wait than that before us," returned Harold.

"But we can see each other every day and be together a good deal of the time," remarked Gracie in low, soothing tones.

"Well, let us have the thing settled, by hearing what father has to say about it," said Max. For at that very moment the captain might be seen approaching their group.

"About what, my son?" he asked, as he took a vacant seat close at hand, for he had overheard the last few words.

"As to the place where our nuptials should be celebrated, sir," returned Max with a little, happy bridegroom laugh.

"Where else but in your homes?" asked his father. "I should like to have both my children married in our house, but Eva and you, I suppose, would prefer to have yours and hers in her home of Fairview."

"No, sir," said Evelyn. "Actually, my very strong wish is to have mine celebrated in my own old home—the house my father built and owned—Crag Cottage."

"Ah, my dear child, that is natural!" returned the captain in a tone of mingled surprise and acquiescence. "I should be loath to stand in the way of such a wish, but I thought you and Lucilla were planning to have but one ceremony for the two couples of you?"

"Yes, sir. Since talking it over we have all four concluded that Crag Cottage would be a suitable place for it, if you do not object."

"It seems to me that there are reasons both for and against it," he said thoughtfully, "but since you four are the ones most nearly concerned, I think it will be only right and kind to let you decide the question among yourselves. But it is growing late in the season, and if the ceremony is to be performed here at the North, it should take place quite soon. Can you make all of the needed preparations in a few days?"

"I think we can," both girls answered to that question affirmatively.

"Very well, then, so far as I am concerned you shall do just as you please. For that matter, you are all of legal age to do so whether you have my permission or not."

At that, all four instantly disclaimed any desire or intention to go at all contrary to his wishes concerning the matter.

"I shall, of course, write at once to my uncle and aunt asking their consent and approval. For, though I am of legal age, I owe them more than that for the great kindness they have shown me ever since the death of my dear father."

"That is a right feeling you have toward them," remarked Captain Raymond in a tone of commendation, "but I have no idea that they will oppose your wishes in the least in this matter."

"No, I am almost sure they will not," she said. "I shall write tonight and hope for a prompt reply. There will be some necessary shopping to do, and New York City will certainly be a good place for that."

"Decidedly," assented the captain, "and you could have no better helpers in that than my wife and her mother."

"And yourself, papa," laughed Lucilla.

"As purse-bearer?" he asked with a smile. "I shall certainly be that and be ready to exercise my taste as regards the choice of the goods."

"And I may be the housekeeper here on the *Dolphin* while you are away on your pleasant errands, I suppose," said Gracie.

"Yes, if you like, daughter," returned the captain.

Harold added, "And I can be your assistant, if you are willing to make use of me."

"To see to it that she does not at all overwork herself," said the captain.

"And what may Chester and I be allowed to do?" queried Max.

"To keep them company, if they desire it, manage the vessel, and keep the children out of mischief, especially from falling overboard. You can also entertain them in harmless ways."

"I think we can do that," said Max, "but how long do you expect to be absent, father? Are we to lie still in the harbor here till you return?"

"Just as you please," said his father. "If you choose to steam along the shores, out into the ocean, or up the river, you have full liberty to do so. All I ask is that you take good care of the children and the vessel."

"Well, sir, I think that with Chester's and Harold's help I can engage to do all that," laughed Max. "Don't you think so, lads?" turning first to one then to the other of the young men. Both returned an affirmative reply. Then they all joined the group of older ladies, told of their plans and purposes, asked for advice, and whether the assistance they wanted in their shopping might be confidently expected.

At first both ladies were surprised that the young people should think of having their weddings before returning home, but, after a little discussion, they all highly approved of the plan and expressed themselves as willing as possible to assist in the shopping and all needful preparations. Then they discussed the question what would be needful or advisable to purchase; what dresses should be made; and where work could be done in the speediest and most approved manner, as it was wisest and best to consider and decide upon these matters before setting out to do their errands.

Evelyn wrote her letter to her uncle and aunt before retiring for the night and had it posted early the next morning. Shortly after breakfast, the shopping party went into the city on their pleasant errand, and a little later the *Dolphin* weighed anchor and steamed out of harbor, going seaward.

The party on its decks was a cheerful, even merry one, Max and Chester rejoicing in the near approach of their long looked-for nuptials. Harold was happy in having full possession for the time of his affianced, and Elsie and Ned Raymond were in merry, youthful sprits, for they loved to be on the yacht and with Brother Max, Uncle Harold, and also Chester with whom they had become almost as free and affectionate as if he were their own brother.

"Where are we going now, Brother Max?" asked Ned.

"I think we will put it to a vote," replied Max. "My idea is that it might be very pleasant to steam along near the shore of the Sound on one side going out and on the other returning. That way, we can get a view of the country on both sides. Gracie, as you are the only lady present, I think you should have the first vote. Shall we do as I have proposed or something different?"

"It sounds very pleasant, Max," replied Gracie, "but I don't wish to decide the question, for I shall enjoy going anywhere in the *Dolphin* with such pleasant company."

"Rather non-committal," laughed Max. "Well, Chester and Harold, what do you two say?"

Both answered that they approved his plan and would like nothing better, and Elsie and Ned exclaimed with enthusiasm that they also would like nothing better.

"A unanimous vote in favor," commented Max. "So the thing is settled."

"And we can settle into some activity," remarked Elsie in a tone of satisfaction. "Uncle Harold, don't you want to tell us about some of the poor wounded or sick fellows you attended to in Cuba?"

"I fear I have not much to tell of them—seeing I have already told so much—except that they were wonderfully brave and patient, full of love for their country and compassion for the downtrodden, inhumanly treated Cubans," replied Dr. Travilla.

"I think our soldiers were very brave, patient, and uncomplaining," said Elsie. "I am very proud of them, especially because they didn't do cruel deeds such as I have read of soldiers of other nations doing in time of war."

"Yes, I think they deserve that commendation," said Harold. "And the attempt of Hobson and his men to block the entrance to Santiago harbor by sinking the *Merrimac* there was brave as brave could be. We certainly have cause to be proud of our soldiers."

"And so we are!" cried Ned enthusiastically. "And," turning toward his brother, "we are just as proud of the brave fellows that were at Manila as of those in Cuba."

"Thank you, young man," returned Max with a bow and a smile. "We certainly have every reason to believe that our doings there have been appreciated by our kind countrymen."

"Brother Max, could you help feeling a little afraid when your ship went into that long channel with its forts and torpedoes?"

"I certainly cannot say that I was entirely free from fear," acknowledged Max, "but I had no desire to escape the danger by giving up my part in the coming fight. I felt that we were on the right side of it—undertaken for the oppressed— and that my Heavenly Father was able to protect me and all of us."

"And He did," exclaimed Elsie in joyful tones. "It was just wonderful how you all escaped being killed, and only a few were slightly wounded."

"It was, indeed," assented Max, "and a great cause for thankfulness."

"Do you like Admiral Dewey, Brother Max?" asked Ned.

"Yes, yes indeed!" was the earnest, smiling reply. "He is determined with his men but very kind-hearted. The man who has been guilty of a fault may be pretty sure of a pardon if he confesses it but not if he tells a falsehood to escape his deserts. Lying is a thing which Dewey utterly detests."

"I wish I could get acquainted with him," said Elsie. "Though I suppose he wouldn't like to be bothered with talking to a little girl of my age."

"I don't know about that," laughed Max. "He is said to be very fond of children."

"Has he any of his own?" she asked with a look of interest.

"One son. He is grown up and is in business."

"Oh, Max, do tell me what sort of folks the Filipinos are?"

"I will do my best," replied Max. "The men are not very tall, but they have good forms and well-shaped heads. Their looks are boyish, and they seem never to grow old. They have black, glossy hair that seldom grows gray. The women are graceful and rather good-looking. They usually wear their hair loose and no hat or bonnet on their heads. Their dress is a satin skirt handsomely embroidered and a waist of pina cloth, having flowing sleeves. They wear a scarf of the finest quality, beautifully embroidered, about their neck and shoulders. An American lady there told me that they often spend years on the embroidery of a single garment, and that she and the other ladies had gone into raptures over that work. But they could seldom secure a specimen. They are a very clean people—bathe a great deal and keep their clothing very clean. Their houses also are kept clean, neat, and tidy. The women sew, spin, weave, and gather thatch to keep the hut in repair. They also catch fish for the family to eat and are skillful at that business. They often carry burdens on their heads, and that makes them erect and graceful. A good many Spaniards and Chinamen have married Filipino women, and the children, called Mestizoes, make good citizens, seeming to inherit the patient industry of the Chinese father and the gentle disposition and dignified self-possession of the Filipino mother. But now I think I have done my share of talking for the present, and I must leave the rest of you to do yours while I see if all is going right with our vessel," added Max, rising and leaving the group as he spoke.

"Uncle Harold, do you know the captain they call 'Fighting Bob'?" asked Ned.

"Slightly," returned his uncle, "and a brave, noble man he is—a naval officer to be proud of. He is perfectly fearless and cool in battle but kind and helpful to conquered foes. He was commander of the *Iowa*, to which the Spanish ship *Vizcaya* surrendered. Her captain, in a speech in Spain, had said that he would tow back the *Iowa* to his king, but he was not able to do so. The *Iowa* drove shell after shell into his vessel until she was in flames and struck her flag.

"'Fighting Bob' sent out his boats to rescue prisoners on the ship and in the water, and he took back to the *Iowa* several officers and 240 men—her captain, Eulate, among them. It is said to have been a horrible scene with so many dead and wounded men and Captain Eulate, limping, and with his head bound up. He saluted as he stepped upon the deck of the *Iowa*, and so did Captain Evans.

"'You are Captain Evans? This is the *Iowa*?' asked Captain Eulate. 'Yes,' said Captain Evans and took Eulate's hand in both of his, shaking it warmly. Eulate stepped back, unbuckled his sword, kissed it, and with the most elegant grace, handed it, hilt forward, to Captain Evans. But he refused to take it, turning the palm of his hand outward and waving it back, at the same time shaking his head—a very emphatic refusal.

"The Spaniards, officers and men, looked on in astonishment. Captain Eulate pressed Captain Evans' hand, and the crew gave Eulate three cheers, for he had fought well and only gave up when his ship was in flames and sinking.

"Just then, a terrific explosion was heard on the *Vizcaya*, which was only a short distance off, and a solid column of smoke went up nearly four thousand feet, it is said, taking the form of a gigantic mushroom. At that, Captain Eulate turned around, pointing with one hand to his ruined ship with the other toward his officers and men. 'Veeski! Veeski!' he cried at the top of his voice, while tears rolled down his cheeks. His men sprang toward him, and many of them kissed his hand. He said in Spanish, 'My brave marines!' and looked away."

"That was certainly a very interesting story, uncle," said Elsie, as Dr. Travilla paused. "I hope there's more of it."

"Oh, yes, please go on, Uncle Harold," said Ned. "Our ships took all the Spanish ones. Didn't they?"

"Yes, the *Maria Teresa* was now a wreck also, and the *Iowa* went to the relief of her drowning and burning men. Admiral Cervera was taken prisoner and brought on board the *Iowa*. When he stepped aboard with his staff, Captain Evans stood with uncovered head, and the marine guard presented arms. Captain Eulate stepped toward him, touched his sword with his hand, and pressed it to his heart, crying out in Spanish and pointing toward Captain Evans, evidently extolling his bravery and generosity. The admiral made a courtly bow to Captain Evans and shook hands with him. The rest of the Spanish officers kissed the hand of the Spanish admiral four times and embraced and kissed Captain Eulate. The men of the crew, too, would now and then see a comrade whom they had supposed dead, and they would fall to embracing and kissing."

"Did Captain Evans thank God for his victory, as Captain Philip did, uncle?" asked Elsie.

"No, but when some one blamed him for not having done so, he said that while preparations were being made for it he found that he was surrounded by boats carrying dying and wounded prisoners and others of the crew of the *Vizcaya*, to the number of 250. 'To leave these men to suffer for want of food and clothing, while I called my men aft to offer prayers, was not my idea of Christianity or religion,' he wrote in reply. 'I preferred to clothe the naked, feed the hungry, and succor the sick, and I am strongly of the opinion that Almighty God has not put a black mark against me on account of it. I do not know whether I shall stand with Captain Philip among the first chosen in the hereafter, but I have this to say in conclusion — that every drop of blood in my body on the afternoon of July third was singing thanks and praise to Almighty God for the victory we had won.'"

"They call Captain Evans 'Fighting Bob.' Don't they, uncle?" asked Ned.

"Yes, but it is said that he does not like it and insists that he is no more of a fighter than very many of his brother officers. But it is really used as an honor to one whom his countrymen admire. But probably he will do no more fighting, as, by his request, he has been detached from the command of the *Iowa* and made a member of the Board of Inspection and Survey. It is a change he is entitled to, having already served more than his term of sea duty."

"Oh, uncle!" said Elsie in a tone of entreaty. "Can't you tell us something more about Captain Philip? I do like him so, because of his being such a good Christian man."

"He is that," said Dr. Travilla emphatically, "and one of the bravest and most modest of men. When asked for his photograph, he replied that he had never had one taken. On being urgently invited to be present at a reception for Lieutenant Hobson given in New York, he shook his head, saying the trial would be too much for him. But I dare say his real reason was a fear that his presence might deprive the young officer of some of the attention and honor due to him."

"Have you ever seen him, uncle?" asked Elsie.

"Yes, once, for a few minutes, and I have heard him described as mild mannered and full of fun. He has a gray mustache, a kindly face, and mild blue eyes, and it is said that he is as fond of his men as they are of him. He said to someone, 'I have a stout ship and a crew of Americans. So had the other captains. That was why we won.' He fairly earned his promotion—first to the rank of commodore then to that of admiral.

"Now you two have taken in a good deal of information. Don't you think it might be well for you to take some exercise in running about the deck?" concluded Uncle Harold in a kindly tone.

Elsie and Ned responded with a cheerful, "Yes, sir! Thank you for the stories," then ran away to carry out his suggestion, Gracie calling after them to be very careful not to go into any dangerous place.

"We won't," Ned called back. "We want to live to go to that double wedding."

"Yes, Ned," said Elsie in a much lower tone, "and we want to buy some handsome presents for the brides. I spoke to mamma about that, and she said she and papa and grandma would give us our turn at the business of shopping. Maybe we can go day after tomorrow, for they expect to come back to the *Dolphin* tomorrow evening, and if the weather is suitable, we can go into the city directly after breakfast the next morning."

"Oh, good!" cried Ned. "Won't it be fun? I hope papa has plenty of money for us to spend, so that we can get something very handsome—jewelry, perhaps. That will be the most suitable and acceptable, I suppose."

"Probably," returned Elsie. "Grandma, papa, and mamma will be the ones to decide."

"Of course," said her brother, "but they'll let us have some say about it, too."

Max and Chester were at the very same moment standing together at some little distance in a friendly discussion of a similar topic—what gifts they should procure for their brides.

"Jewelry of some sort would, I suppose, be considered the most appropriate," remarked Chester in an inquiring tone.

"That is my idea," returned Max. "I believe the majority of ladies can hardly have too much of it—though I have never noticed Eva cared very much about it. I think, however, that Lu does. I know that some years ago she had a very strong desire for more jewelry than father deemed best for her."

"Tastes differ," sagely remarked Chester, "and I wish to give her whatever she would prefer."

"Certainly," said Max. "That is right and kind and just my feeling in regard to my gift for Eva."

"Well," said Chester, "fortunately we do not need to decide the question until we see what the jewelers and other merchants have to offer."

"Shall we go together to make our selections?" asked Max.

"I should like to do so, if it suits you, and to have your father along—Cousins Elsie and Violet also, if they feel inclined to go."

"Yes, indeed!" said Max. "They both have excellent taste and judgment, and I don't know any one whose opinion on the subject I should consider more valuable."

"Nor do I," responded Chester. "We are very fortunate in our lady friends, and I may add in our gentlemen also, Max, your father especially."

"Thank you," returned Max with a smile of gratification. "I think there is not a more perfect man and gentleman anywhere to be found, but that may be because I am his son."

"Oh, no! Not altogether, at any rate," said Chester. "For you are by no means alone in your favorable opinion."

"No, I flatter myself that I am not. Ah! Do you see how earnestly Harold and Gracie are talking together? I shouldn't wonder if they are upon the very same subject we have just been discussing."

"Quite likely. It seems to be the most important subject for the members of our party at present."

"Yes. By the way, Chester, we are hurrying matters so that we can hardly hope or expect to have very many of our Southern relatives and friends to witness the ceremony."

"No, I suppose we can't. But we might invite them to visit us in our house as soon after we get there as they please," laughed Chester.

"True enough!" exclaimed Max, looking highly pleased at the thought. "How delightful it will be to entertain them there."

"So I think, and you know how I have wanted a home for that, as well as for my own private enjoyment," commented Chester.

"I have had some rather severe attacks of homesickness since I left my father's house for the Naval Academy, so I think I can understand your feelings," Max said with a smile. "And I expect to be somewhat envious of you and Lu some months hence when I have to leave my wife and home to go—perhaps—to the other side of the world."

"Yes, Max, when I think of that I am sorry for you and for ourselves that we must be so often deprived of your pleasant society."

They were steaming along within sight of the shore, and just at that moment the children came running to ask Max some question about what could be seen there. He listened and replied very kindly, Chester now and then taking part in their pleasant talk.

The day and evening passed pleasantly to all on board. The children retired at their accustomed early hour, Gracie helping little Elsie in preparing for her couch lest the dear, little sister should miss her mamma too sorely and wet her pillow with tears. Ned considered himself almost a man now and quite fit to do without any attention in that line. "I do miss mamma," Elsie said, as she laid herself down in the berth, "but it is very nice to share this stateroom with you for once, Gracie dear."

"And I am very glad to have you do so," replied Gracie. "I shall not miss Lu half so much with you in her place."

"It's nice and kind of you to say that," replied Elsie with a loving look and smile. "Don't feel as if you must come to bed as early as I do, but you must go back and enjoy Brother Max, Uncle Harold, and Chester a little longer. I am sure they want you to."

"Well, then I'll kiss you goodnight, you darling little sister, and go back to them for perhaps another hour," Gracie said, accompanying her words with a tender caress.

She found the gentlemen still on deck where she had left them, and they gave her no reason to doubt that her society was welcome to them.

An hour was spent in cheerful chat and some singing of appropriate songs and hymns. Then they bade goodnight, and all retired to their staterooms, Max having first attended to all his duties as captain of the vessel.

The night passed quietly, and the next morning all woke rested and refreshed, ready to enjoy their breakfast. After that, the walks and talks upon deck varied with resting in steamer chairs while chatting and gazing out upon the water and land, out of sight of which they seldom were. The weather was all that could be desired, and they rejoiced in that fact for both themselves and their friends, the shoppers.

The latter came on board soon after the yacht had come to anchor again in New York harbor. Their bright, cheerful faces told at once of success with what had been undertaken and of satisfaction with their purchases. Their tongues speedily repeated the pleasant story of beautiful silks, satins, laces, and other trimmings. In this family circle, they did not care to make a secret of their needful or desirable preparations for the approaching ceremony.

All passed the night on the vessel, Violet remarking that one night at the best of hotels was quite enough for her. She felt so much more at home on their own delightful yacht. Shortly after breakfast, the children were taken into the city to select their bridal gifts, their father and mother going along with them. Gracie, in compliance with a suggestion from her father, was quite willing to entrust the selection of her gifts to him and mamma, shopping being always wearisome work for her.

Grandma Elsie, Evelyn, and Lucilla remained on the vessel with Gracie to take a good rest, while the young men went in search of their gifts for the brides that were to be.

"So, tell me, how many dresses did you have fitted?" asked Gracie.

"Two apiece," replied her sister, "our wedding gowns and one other for each of us. The others were expressed home at once to be made up by our own dressmakers, so that they may be ready to wear by the time we return or soon after."

"A very good plan, I think," said Gracie. "Eva, have you heard from your uncle and aunt in reply to your note the other day?"

"Yes," Evelyn replied with a smile, "and I am happy to say that they highly approve of our plans and purposes — not even bidding me beware of the truth of the old saying, 'Marry in haste and repent in leisure.' They have promised to have everything in readiness for us and our ceremony. Isn't it good of them?"

"Very nice and kind, I think," said Gracie. "How favorably everything seems to go with you! I am very glad for you both."

"Thank you," said Eva. "We might even make a triple wedding of it if your father would only consent, Gracie."

"Oh, no! I don't wish it. Father is right, I know. He always is, and I don't want to leave him yet for anybody."

"And you are entirely right in that, my dear," said Grandma Elsie. "I can see that, although I should dearly love to gain possession of my new little daughter at once."

"It is very nice and kind of you, Grandma Elsie, to be so ready to claim me for your own," Gracie returned, happy tears shining in her eyes.

"Ah, I fear your father might see that in a different light," returned Grandma Elsie with one of her sweet smiles. "I think he would prefer to keep you all his own, and I cannot blame him. Now, girls," turning to the others, "suppose we make a list of the friends and relatives who should be invited to your wedding, so that that matter can be promptly attended to."

The girls gave a ready assent, and the list was presently prepared.

"Now I have been thinking," Eva said, as they finished, "that as October is so delightful a month, even up here on the Hudson, we might as well take a little more time for our preparations. We can spend it at Crag Cottage, and that would make it possible for our friends to attend the ceremony, should they choose to come. You could spare that much more time from your home. Couldn't you, Grandma Elsie?"

"Easily, and I think it a very good idea. If anything like the entire number of our friends should come, you would not have sleeping accommodations for nearly all of them. The hotels in the neighborhood are, I think, closed or will be by that time, but a noon wedding would enable guests to come in the morning and leave before night."

"Oh, that's a capital idea, Grandma Elsie!" exclaimed Lucilla. "Don't you think so, Eva?"

"I do, and I think every one else will," returned Eva joyously. "Then our wedding gifts can be shown at the cottage, packed, and sent home afterward in plenty of time to get there before we do. For as you all already know, we four are to take a bridal trip to Niagara Falls before going home."

When the shoppers returned and were told of this plan, they one and all highly approved. So it was decided upon; the necessary preparations were promptly made; and the invitations made up and sent off.

The children were in high spirits, delighted with the purchases they had made. The older people seemed equally satisfied with theirs, though their report was given in quieter fashion. Some of the smaller gifts the purchasers brought with them, but the others were to be sent to Crag Cottage and after the wedding from there to the brides' home. After some little discussion of the plan, an immediate return to Crag Cottage was decided upon, and presently the yacht was steaming up the river.

❦❧❦❧❦❧❦❧

CHAPTER SIXTEENTH

IT WAS QUITE A pleasant and happy party that gathered around the breakfast table at Crag Cottage the next morning, and it was a bountiful and excellent meal they found spread before them.

Mrs. Elsie Leland—acting mistress of the house for the present—was highly pleased with the new arrangements planned for the double wedding.

"The extension of the time allotted for the preparations will make it much easier to carry them out," she said, "while invited guests will have more time for the carrying out of theirs. I doubt if many of them would think it worthwhile to take so long and expensive a journey even to see that interesting sight—a double wedding."

"I dare say not," said her husband. "Chester, do you expect your brother and your two sisters to be here?"

"Hardly, the time being so short and the journey so long. Frank, I heard a short time ago, has now found a ladylove down there, which will be likely to keep him away. Each of my sisters, as you probably know, has a young child—Maud, indeed, has two and Sydney has one. They would probably want neither to bring the little ones along nor leave them behind."

"No, I suppose none of them will hardly want to journey so far for such a short visit and will think it too late in the season for a long one," remarked Grandma Elsie.

"Yes. I also fear that will keep Uncle Horace and Aunt Rose from joining us, though they are no farther away than Philadelphia," said Chester.

"And, as Grandpa sometimes says, they are not so young as they once were," said Mrs. Leland. "We would be delighted to have them with us, but we can scarcely hope for it."

"No," said Violet, "and most of our relatives and friends, having had their summer outings, returned home, and settled down again, can hardly be expected to start out on so long a journey for so short a bit of entertainment."

"Especially as there are a number of people getting married every day," laughed Lucilla.

"Yes," said Harold with a smile, "it is a very common occurrence."

The two weeks passed quickly and happily away, the older ones attending to necessary preparations and the younger ones filling up much of the time with pleasant little excursions up and down the river in the yacht or walks, rides, and drives on land.

The wedding presents began to come in. The captain's principal gift they knew was their joint home on his estate, Woodburn, but there were a number of minor ones in the way of silver for their tables, Sevres china, napery, cut glass, and bric-a-brac. The gifts of Elsie and Ned consisted of similar articles. Gracie's gift, chosen by her father and Mamma Vi, was a gold bracelet for each ornamented with precious stones. Each lover had visited Tiffany's and bought for his bride a very handsome ornament called a sunburst—a star of diamonds to be worn as locket or brooch. They were presented on the morning of the wedding, and the girls were delighted with them, as they were with Harold's gift—a very beautiful opal ring to each.

It was nearing ten o'clock on the night before the wedding, and Captain Raymond was taking his usual stroll back and forth upon the porch before retiring when Lucilla came to him for their usual bit of goodnight chat so pleasant to them both. He put his arm about her and held her close to his heart, as he had so often done before. For a moment neither spoke, but then she said sobbingly, "Oh, father, my dear father, this is the last time! How can I bear it? Oh, how can I bear it! How can I leave you, even for Chester, whom I do love dearly?"

"No, dear child," he said in tones tremulous with emotion, "it need not be the last time. We shall be near enough to see and embrace each other very often while God spares our lives, and we will not love each other less because we are not living all the time under the same roof."

"No, papa. No, indeed! Oh, I could never bear it if it wasn't for knowing that! You have been such a good, kind, wise, and loving father to me. Oh, I wish I had always been the good, obedient biddable child I ought to have been."

"Yes, daughter, dear, I know it. I know you do, while I often wish I had been more patient and gentle—less stern with you. But let us forgive and forget, and each try in the future to be all to the other that could be desired. My own dear, dear child! 'The Lord bless thee: the Lord make His face to shine upon thee, and be gracious unto thee: the Lord lift up His countenance upon thee, and give thee peace.'"

"Thank you, my dear, dear father," she said. "That is such a sweet blessing, and I do so love to hear it from your lips. Oh, I can never be thankful enough that I have a Christian father!"

"Nor I for the good hope that my dear eldest daughter is a true servant with me of the same blessed Master. Now let us say goodnight, for it is time you were preparing for your rest."

Most of the invited guests except a few who would arrive in the morning had come, but, by sending the young gentlemen and lads to sleep in the yacht, room had been made for all.

The ceremony took place the next day at high noon—the brides, the gifts, the house bedecked with flowers, all looking very lovely. A grand wedding breakfast followed. Then bridal dresses were exchanged for traveling suits, handsome and becoming, and the newly married couples, accompanied by Gracie and Harold, went aboard the *Dolphin*, which carried them to the city, where they would take the cars for Niagara. Harold and Gracie saw them on the train, waved good-bye to them as it started, and then returned on the yacht to Crag Cottage.

A few days later, the *Dolphin* was again speeding southward, carrying her owner and his family including Mrs. Travilla, her son Harold, and the Lelands to their homes. They had a delightful voyage and arrived at their destination in fine health and spirits. But that was not the last trip made by the yacht that season. Within a fortnight, she was again steaming up the Hudson, and in the harbor of the city where the bridal party had left her, they found her again lying at anchor one day when the train bearing them on their return from the west came rushing into the station.

"Oh, it really seems something like getting home!" Lucilla exclaimed as she stepped upon the deck. "But father did not come!" she added with a slight sigh of disappointment, glancing about in the vain hope of catching sight of the manly form and face she loved so well.

"No, Mrs. Dinsmore, but you'll be sure to get sight of the captain when you reach the other end of the voyage," said Mr. Bailey, the temporary skipper, coming forward with a bow and a smile.

"And the voyage will be but a short one if the weather continues good," remarked Max, offering a hand to Bailey in cordial greeting and introducing his bride.

"Yes," said Bailey, taking in his hand the hand she offered and looking at her with admiring eyes. "I used to know her pretty well as Miss Leland. I wish you both a great deal of happiness and prosperity. And you and your bride the same, Mr. Dinsmore," shaking hands with Chester in his turn. "I think, ladies and gentlemen, you will find everything shipshape in the salon and staterooms. The captain was very particular about all that."

"Yes," said Evelyn, "and now that we are here on the dear old yacht, I feel that the discomforts of travel by rail are happily gotten rid of. Everything is so clean, quiet, and homelike here."

"I think it is delightful," said Lucilla. "Only I am disappointed that father did not come."

"No doubt it was having too many other things to attend to that prevented him," said Max. "And doubtless he will meet us at the wharf when we land there."

The weather was all that could be desired. The yacht was in fine condition, and in due time, they anchored in the harbor of their own city and presently landed to find a number of the dear ones waiting for them. Captain Raymond was there with his entire family, and Lucilla had scarcely stepped ashore ere she found herself in his arms, his kisses of fatherly love falling fast upon her upturned lips and cheeks.

"How glad I am to have you here again, my darling," he said in tender tones. "I hope you have enjoyed your trip and come back to me feeling well and strong?"

"Oh, yes, father dear. Yes, indeed! And we are so, so glad to be with you again! I could never, never live without my father."

"That is pretty much as I feel about my eldest daughter," he returned with a smile, repeating his caresses.

Then Eva must take her turn, and the son and son-in-law each received a cordial grasp and shake of the hand. Then joyous greetings were exchanged with the Lelands, Violet, Elsie, and Ned. The Woodburn and Fairview carriages were there, and nearby stood another—a two-seated, very handsome vehicle with a pair of fine, spirited-looking grays attached. Greetings over, the captain led the way to the equipage, and turning with a kind, fatherly smile toward the bridal party, "Here, my children," he said, "is a gift from your father to held and used—enjoyed, too, I trust—by the four of you in common."

"Father, I'm afraid you are doing too much for us!" exclaimed Max with emotion.

"A grand, good gift, sir, for which I heartily thank you," said Chester warmly.

"Dear father, don't ruin yourself by heaping so many, many gifts upon us," cried Lucilla, turning, and putting her hand in his, while Evelyn said, with starting tears that it was really too much.

"No, I am perfectly able to afford it, my dears, and I shall be very glad if it adds to your enjoyment of your new home," said the generous giver. "Get in now, drive over to your new home, and see if everything about the house and grounds has been arranged to suit your taste."

They obeyed and found the carriage, as they afterward said, the easiest, most comfortable one they had ever ridden in and the horses the finest of thoroughbreds.

"These are grand fellows, Max. I'll warrant your father has spent no trifle on their purchase," remarked Chester, as they sped onward with easy, graceful motion.

"Just what I think," said Max. "Indeed, no more generous man than he ever lived."

"I only hope he won't ruin himself by heaping expensive gifts and favors upon us," said Evelyn.

"I hope not, indeed!" sighed Lucilla with a slight tremble in her tones.

"Don't be anxious and troubled about it, sister mine," said Max very kindly. "I happen to know that father has abundant means. And being so generous of nature it is a delight to him to give — especially to his wife and children."

"What a dear, good father he is! It is just a delight to me that I may call him that now," said Evelyn.

Their carriage reached its destination some minutes ahead of the captain's, and they immediately alighted and gazed about them with wondering and delighted eyes. So many improvements had been made since last they saw the place — trees and flowers, lovely and fragrant, having been transplanted from other places to adorn this. They wandered here and there, expressing in looks and joyous exclamations, admiration, gratitude, and delight.

They had hardly made acquaintance with all the beauties of the place when the other carriage drove up and the rest of the family joined them. Then, as the captain afterward said, they well-nigh overwhelmed him with the extravagant outpouring of their admiration, gratitude, and delight at the changes.

"I am glad that you are all so well pleased," he said in return. "My wife and I have greatly enjoyed this labor of love—the overseeing and directing of these improvements. That they find such favor with you all more than repays us. But, come, let us go inside and see how well you are satisfied with things there."

He led the way as he spoke, and they found themselves in a wide hall with a broad and easy stairway leading to the rooms above. On either side on that floor, they found large, elegantly furnished rooms—parlors, libraries, dining rooms—a set for each little family. There were beautiful lace curtains at the windows, handsome paintings handsomely framed on the walls—many of them presents from Grandma Elsie and the others of the Ion family and Violet's relatives on the neighboring estates—and other gifts and adornments too numerous to mention.

The young folks had decided to call their place Sunnyside, and so lovely was it that the name seemed very appropriate. The upper rooms were found scarcely less attractive in themselves or their furnishings than the lower ones. A grand dinner was in course of preparation in Lucilla's own kitchen, and presently all sat down to it, being served in her dining room. After that, the whole party went over to Woodburn, as not one of them felt satisfied without a peep at it—the dear, old home all loved so well.

The End

Invite little Elsie Dinsmore™ Doll Over to Play!

Breezy Point Treasures' Elsie Dinsmore™ Doll brings Martha Finley's character to life in this collectible eighteen-inch all-vinyl play doll produced in conjunction with Lloyd Middleton Dolls.

The Elsie Dinsmore™ Doll comes complete with authentic Antebellum clothing and a miniature Bible. This series of books emphasizes traditional family values so your and your child's character will be enriched as have millions since the 1800's.

Doll available from:

Breezy Point Treasures, Inc.
124 Kingsland Road
Hayneville, GA 31036 USA

Call for details on ordering:

1-888-487-3777

or visit our website at
www.elsiedinsmore.com